Out of the Red and into the Black

By Shane A. Ahalt Sr.

Check out the bookables
for the cutest
character bookmarks.

Out of the Red and into the Black
Copyright © 2019 by Shane Ahalt Sr.

This book is a work of fiction, the characters, incidents, and dialogues are products of the author's imagination and are not to be construed as real. Any resemblance to actual persons, living or dead is entirely coincidental.

Dedication

To everyone that has ever called me brother, friend, or family, I thank each of you for letting me be a part of your life.

To my father for setting the example and being my inspiration to be the best man I can be.

To my boys, Ryan and Aaron, for giving me the motivation to be a father you can be proud of.

Finally, to the love of my life, Alicia. I'm a better person because of you. I love you more than you will ever know.

Table of Contents

Chapter 1
A Debt Is Paid

He awoke, trying to shake the fog in his head. His vision was blurred and his head was groggy. *Did I drink that much last night? Where am I?* he thought. His surroundings were strange yet familiar. Wondering where he was a fleeting thought because it was overruled by the pain. The agonizing pain in his left knee overrode all of his other senses and thoughts. As the fog in his head thinned, he realized he was tied to a chair and couldn't move his arms or legs. The shape in front of him seemed familiar but out of place. He heard his wife's voice emitting from the female shape in front of him. And there was a smell, a familiar odor that was unidentifiable through the fog in his head. But the knee. It was killing him. The pain was so great that this man that never cried or wept because of pain, moaned in agony.

Gasoline. That was the smell... and pain. The pain in that knee was so excruciating that it dominated all other thought.

Somehow, someone had gotten the best of him. He was stuck and, as much as he struggled, he couldn't break free. How did he get here? Had he been knocked out or had he been drugged? It was clear to him now that this was his bedroom. He recognized the nightstand that normally rested next to his side of the bed, but it was on the floor next to the female shape in front of him. The fog was lifting now and his blurred vision began to clear. He realized what the shape in front of him was now. The shape was Tammy, his wife, with her wrists and legs tied to hooks in the ceiling and floor. The smell of gasoline permeated the air, but he didn't know why. And the PAIN!!

"I want you to watch this! From what I have seen, you like to watch things. Your actions and her inaction have brought the wrath of God upon you," the assailant said as calmly as someone ordering Chinese carryout. This bastard wore no mask or gloves and moved methodically with a purpose. Eric heard what sounded like a chainsaw, but as this sick son of a bitch came back into view, Eric was able to see the weed-whacker in this man's hands. The gasoline smell now made sense. The lunatic showed no emotion in his face when he walked toward Tammy with the weed-whacker in hand. He pulled the trigger to get the yard tool to full speed. Then he used the tool to slash Tammy's outer thigh. This weed-whacker was the same tool Eric had used every other weekend during the spring and summer to manicure his lawn. But now, this tool was being used to torture the love of Eric's life. "Eric!" she screamed. "Help me!"

"I'll fucking kill you," Eric tried to yell, but his screams were muffled. He was desperately pulling against the duct tape holding his wrists and ankles to the chair. He couldn't watch. Not being able to do anything about his wife's pain was too much and watching was torture. He turned his head. All the while, he was working against the restraints on his wrist. He felt a rage he had never felt before and that rage fueled every cell in his body except his left knee. In that knee, there was nothing but PAIN!

"Watch!" the assailant commanded.

"I won't, but when I get free, I'm going to kill you," Eric tried to reply. Again, his voice was muffled.

The assailant put down the weed-whacker and removed a knife from the sheath attached to his belt. This knife was huge, like a Bowie knife. He moved to Eric and cut off his left ear with his knife. "Watch, or more body parts will be removed," he coldly stated as he moved back to Tammy and the weed-whacker.

An odd thought popped into Eric's head. He was taken back to his childhood and a few times he hurt a body part when his father was around. If Eric went to his dad and said his foot hurt, for instance, his father would punch him in the arm and say, "How does your foot feel now?" Surprisingly, the pain in his foot or whatever body part ached would be overridden by the pain in his arm.

Eric's knee no longer mattered; the missing ear overrode that pain much the way his father's shot in the arm did in his childhood.

The assailant pulled the trigger and brought the tool up to speed. He looked at Eric and said one word. "Watch." But Eric couldn't. He turned his head away and continued to work to get his wrists free.

The assailant seemed angry, although the emotions his face showed were minimal. He walked to Eric, pulled out some duct tape, and pushed Eric's right cheek against the back of the chair so Eric could only look to the right. Then he duct-taped Eric's head in that position so he couldn't turn his head. Next, he turned the chair to make it so Eric could only look at Tammy. During all this time, Tammy moaned in agony. Finally, the assailant pulled out a box cutter. He grabbed Eric's right eyelid and pulled it away from his eye and used the razor sharp blade to cut it off. Eric screamed, but the assailant wasn't fazed. He did the same to Eric's left eyelid and said, "Now you have no choice but to watch."

The sweat and blood poured from his forehead and dripped directly into his eyes, causing him more pain. He could feel the duct tape losing its grip slowly but surely as a result of the sweat. He knew that it would be only a matter of minutes before he'd be free. Then this sick son of a bitch would pay, if he could see him.

The moans from Tammy sickened him. *Oh, this son of a bitch will pay*, he thought.

Tammy's screams appeared to mean as much to the torturer as that of a dog barking in the distance. Tammy moaned continually and the moans and cries of Eric's name were only interrupted by the screams resulting from the more deep slices from the weed whacker. There were easily twenty such cuts on her now, from the top of her head to the gashes on her blood-soaked feet. The worst seemed to be a slash across her face encompassing her nose and what remained of her left eye. The assailant was careful not to cut any major arteries and, although the cuts were deep, none of them would prove to be fatal if Tammy ever made it to find some medical care. Feasibly, he could inflict this type of torture for hours and not kill her.

Eric's eyes hurt. He tried to close his eyes, but nothing happened. There was just the pain. The great pain emanated from his eyes. His ear and knee were no longer a concern. Just his eyes and killing this "mutha fucker" that dared mess with him and his wife.

There was no sign of Tyler, Eric's son, and the assailant hadn't mentioned him. If this psychopath was going to kill him and his wife, he wasn't going to give up any opportunity to save himself.

"The boy. You want the boy," he tried to say through the tape.

The assailant seemed to understand through the duct tape. He stopped, walked over to Eric, and ripped the tape off. Even though the tape was starting to come loose, the adhesive pulling the hairs out of his perfectly trimmed goatee was nearly as painful as his recently separated ear, but this pain was fleeting.

"What did you say?" the assailant asked.

"The boy, take him. Just let us be."

"Oh, I will take him and I am going to let you be...when I am done."

The assailant placed a fresh piece of tape over Eric's mouth.

The tape on Eric's wrists and feet was not as fresh, and through his struggling, he could feel it coming free. With a loosening of the duct tape on his wrists, Eric really believed he could break free… and soon.

Eric struggled. "Stop! If it's me you want, then come get me." He tried to shout, but the words were muffled.

Why was he in this position? He was convinced that this had to do with his true profession of drug dealing, not his "legit" job as a clerk at the local auto parts store, but the comments about liking to watch were a clue. This had to do with his secret life. He could feel the tape starting to give way.

It wouldn't be long now. He knew no help would be coming. He lived on a secluded piece of land. He liked it that way for multiple reasons and he knew from experience that screams from him and his wife would go unanswered.

The man walked up to him, took a tomahawk out of his backpack, and clobbered Eric's right knee. Eric cried out in agony. Again, the screams were muffled. The man returned to torturing Tammy.

This fresh pain overruled the rest. He imagined the earlier pain in his left knee was from the same sort of damage that was just done to his right and that pain was enough. Eric started to fade.

"Oh no you don't." The assailant walked over to him and broke up an ammonia capsule, better known as smelling salts, and placed it under Eric's nose. Eric's head tried to jolt back, but it couldn't overcome the force of the duct tape. Either way, he was fully conscious now.

Despite the pain, Eric continued to try to work his left hand free. He was almost there, he could feel it coming loose. *Oh, the sick son of a bitch is going to pay.*

Finally, it was loose. As he pulled his left hand free, he heard a strange sound, a muffled "BANG" and, as the pain in his groin started to register, the assailant stopped what he was doing. The sound Eric heard was that of .410 shotgun wrapped in a pillow going off, shooting him in his groin area. When Eric freed his wrist, it pulled a string tied to this gun and aimed with the intention of removing his manhood, or at least damage it greatly. This was clearly the work of someone sickly ingenious and the cue for the executioner to finish the job. He used the knife to cut open what was left of Eric's jeans and stabbed Eric in the leg next to his knee, causing Eric to scream in pain, and ran the blade up Eric's leg to what was left of his genitals and kicked Eric's chair over.

Next, he took a can of lighter fluid from his pocket and used it to douse both Eric and Tammy. Then he lit a match and tossed it into Eric's lap to start the "cleansing fire."

As the flames rose all over Eric and moved towards Tammy, the executioner stood and watched as Eric used his free arm to try to crawl to Tammy. He could hear Eric's muffled screams as he was engulfed in fire, then Tammy's. The torturer watched, and before Eric's screams diminished, he used the fire extinguisher to put out the human candles. He left them there alive, but barely, to suffer in great agony. He slowly walked out of the room and down the hall to the deeply sleeping and drugged child. He lifted him in his arms and left through the downstairs exit. His debt was paid and he was now out of the red and into the black.

Chapter 2
A Victim Is Found

Tyler Creasy was a normal child, by all accounts, and had a normal childhood. He loved to play video games, he played baseball at the local ballpark, and he was a very good student.

His family was one that wanted for nothing, not rich, but one that lived comfortably. Tyler was afforded all the trappings of an upper middle class household and country living. He had an X-box game system, a four-wheeler to ride around the property. He and his father went on hunting and fishing trips. His mother didn't need to work outside of the home and this family attended church service every Sunday morning and, often, the Sunday afternoon session as well. From all appearances, this was a happy child raised in a good wholesome family. That all changed on his ninth birthday. That was when the horror started.

At first, it was the odd touches by, of all people, his mother. Since early childhood, Tyler would climb into bed with his parents after a nightmare and cuddle against his mother. One night, while cuddling with her, she touched him on his "little bird."

That first time, Tyler thought it was an accident, but that wasn't the last time. Over time, things progressed and Tyler's mother was more intimate with him than any mother should be with her son. To make matters worse, this was all witnessed by Eric and, eventually, this sad excuse of a father and a man joined in.

In only a few months, Tyler had gone from a happy-go-lucky kid to one being tormented by full-scale sexual abuse and the inherent guilt associated with it. He dared not betray his parents as they continually preached the word of God from the Bible. His father would say "Ephesians 6:1, Children, obey your parents for this is right." Never did Tyler hear the words, "Lead not your children to wrath." Or any other verse telling him what was happening to him was wrong. In his soul, he knew it wasn't right. He could see it in his mother's eyes, though she did nothing to stop his father; and, he was obedient to his parents, their advances, and their wishes.

The abuse continued for a number of years. At first, it was once a week or so, but as the years grew, so did the frequency. By his twelfth birthday, the incidents were daily occurrences. Each time his father came to him, Tyler would escape into his mind and find himself in the world of *Assassin's Creed*, where he could become an assassin linked through his DNA to an assassin from the past. He would slip into this make-believe land and move catlike from building to building, killing those that tried to kill him. Oftentimes, he would imagine his father was one of those men he killed in the game

The worst of the abuse occurred when Tyler's dad would invite his "friends" over to participate. The "friends" consisted of other children, both boys and girls, and adult men and women who would take turns abusing him or them and watch them as they were forced to interact with each other.

When Tyler was thirteen years old, he was on his Xbox playing a *Call of Duty*, one of his other favorite games, and talking to another child online. His parents didn't know that he had "hacked" into the Wi-Fi and he never played online when they were home. The kid was talking about the Sandusky incidents at Penn State University. He said Jerry Sandusky was a sick man for molesting the children entrusted to his care and that the children would be scarred for life.

With the barrier of face-to-face conversation removed, people spoke freely on Xbox about their prejudices, desires, and the goings on of current events. People expressed themselves without restrictions because of the anonymity and freedom from consequences of their statements.

Through a long conversation, he found out that the incidents the other boy was talking about were just like those he was experiencing at home with his father, mother, and his father's friends. The tone in his voice was all the other "boy" needed in order to realize that something was going on.

The "boy" on the other end wasn't a boy. It was a man, Brian Smart, twenty-eight years in age. Brian was a handsome man of darkish complexion with deep blue eyes. If you looked closely, you could see the blue was broken up by brown wedges at the bottom of his irises. He was often mistaken for being Hispanic, Mediterranean, or Middle Eastern descent. However, he truly didn't know his full heritage. His parents never told him and they were no longer around to ask. By his looks, he surmised that he was African American and something else, perhaps Native American or Mexican or maybe even Caucasian.

Brian was a computer programmer who worked in the FBI's Cyber Crimes Division. He demonstrated great computer skills as a young man. He went to a local community college on his own dime at the age of nineteen. He worked his way through school and never took a handout from anyone. Brian had issues with trusting people and chose to do everything for himself. While in school, he became an expert in computer programming from C++, to JavaScript, Visual Basic, and even some of the antiques like FORTRAN and Machine Language. The ones and zeroes spoken by computers were second nature to Brian and he soon outgrew his teachers. He would often ask questions that they were not able to answer. He would develop software, hacks, and use methodologies that the professors at the community college weren't able to generate on their own and could barely comprehend.

Although he didn't test well on the ACT or SAT, and his grades in other classes were not anything extraordinary, Brian's computer savvy earned him titles such as "genius" or "savant" when people discussed his abilities. One professor acknowledged his own shortcomings when compared to Brian's abilities and brought Brian to the attention of the school's president. It turned out the president had close ties with MIT and he was able to get Brian an interview of sorts via a programming challenge. Brian's abilities earned him acceptance to MIT easily.

Well before he graduated, many companies were clamoring for his services. He was offered salaries in the six-figure range before he had a degree. However, his past experiences and an internship with the Bureau made it clear that his destiny lay with the FBI's Cyber Crimes Division. When he "applied" for the job, the interview was a mere formality.

Brian's talents allowed him to program a portable box that acted as a filter as he spoke online and played video games on Xbox. His favorite game to play was *Call of Duty*. It seemed that game had the most participants and chatter. Also, it was fun to play. His real purpose for playing was to find that one victim out there; the one that no one knew about; the one that those at the Bureau had no clue about; the one that wasn't being posted on the dark web of the internet.

Brian found victim after victim. He'd find these children online. He was amazed at what children would tell each other after they had gained each other's trust while playing a video game. Children would tell all sorts of things to an individual they had never met. He surmised that some of it was trust and the other part was anonymity.

When Brian was able to find out about Tyler, he used his backdoor to the FBI's Cyber Crimes tracking program. The program was developed by someone he knew well: himself. From the back door, no one at the FBI would ever know he was in the system and he had full access to every case under investigation and every individual under suspicion from every FBI field office. It turned out that, unlike the other victims he had found while playing *Call of Duty*, the help for Tyler was not coming anytime soon, as no one in the FBI or an agency that reported to the FBI knew about his secret. Tyler would be the one; the one that would get Brian out of the red and into the black so to speak. Tyler would allow Brian to repay his debt.

When Brian was on Xbox, he went by the gamertag of SurfGod234, although he had never successfully been surfing. He had visited California as a teenager and tried surfing once, and even though he was an exceptional athlete, he couldn't get the hang of it. Still, he liked the idea of becoming a surfer. He liked to think that, maybe if his life had been different, he could have made surfing work. That was the source of his gamertag.

Tyler always called Brian SurfBro. That was his own version of SurfGod. Tyler just couldn't bring himself to call anyone God. Perhaps that was due to the reverence he felt towards God or maybe it was because of his anger with God for letting him be sexually abused.

Everything Brian was taught as a teenager would come into play. Every step he was forced to memorize would come out. Shutting down his emotions, as he had practiced so many times before, would be needed. No physical training would be required. He was in shape. He never missed a morning five-mile run, no matter what the weather. In addition to his runs, he spent three days a week training on a heavy bag and he spent two days a week with crossfit workouts. At twenty-eight, Brian was in better shape than most professional athletes. He was a skilled boxer and even trained in the holds and kicks required to fight MMA style. He knew how to make tranquilizers out of common plants. He knew how to stalk, plan, and attack his prey. He could shoot a quarter at ten yards with either a .45 caliber handgun or a compound bow. He could shoot his AR-15 rifle with the precision of a police sniper, although he didn't think he'd need that skill for this mission. Brian knew how to hunt. He was trained, kept up his skills, and had prepared for this for roughly fourteen years now. This was going to be quick, precise, and he would take no pleasure in his actions other than the enjoyment of saving a child and knowing his debt was paid.

The first step was to verify what he believed was true. Using his internet tracking skills, he was able to find Tyler's address just outside Memphis, Tennessee. A quick check of Google Earth allowed him to see the lay of the land. The house was on a secluded tract of land that was about ten acres in area. The house sat nearly a quarter mile off the road and there was vacant land surrounding it for hundreds of yards with the exception of one house that was over 200 yards away, and that was through trees, a six-foot privacy fence, and assorted brush and undergrowth. If you wanted to be away from it all, this house was where you wanted to live. If you wanted to hide something, this house was perfect for that as well.

Brian realized that scoping out the house would be easy. The house's seclusion would allow for him to pick a spot and remain there for hours on end and not have to worry about nosy neighbors or a random police car wondering about his motives. He also realized that, if he were discovered, an escape wouldn't be as easy as jumping in a car and driving away, but he was prepared for that eventuality.

He had some vacation time on the books. So this would be "his chance to go visit the Land of Rhythm and Blues, the home of Elvis and the Civil Rights museum." The coincidence of his arrival in Memphis and what he was about to do shouldn't be connected. However, he knew he'd need to cover his tracks just in case his actions drew suspicion. There would be no hotels and all their cameras to track his comings and goings. He needed something with less observations and more freedom to come and go at all times of the day and night. At first, he thought of a bed and breakfast but realized a midnight run, a late night arrival, or a full day's absence might draw some questions. He needed to be free from anyone's concerns… a campground. That was it. He looked for an RV park in the vicinity. His plan was to take his RV that he had set it up as a Command Center with computers, GPS trackers, monitors, and all of the equipment needed to conduct a surveillance operation. His personal RV would make most small-town police departments jealous.

Once there, he would use his Zero DS electric motorcycle to get around. The advantage of the motorcycle was that it was quiet, which drew no attention, and it was able to be driven on and off road. The drawback was its range. His campground would have to be within seventy miles, unless he found a place to get a recharge. Brian found a campground about twenty-six miles from the Creasy residence. It would do. If he needed a charge from somewhere, he was usually able to get one from a local Waffle House or any diner. Curiosity about the bike usually gained him access to an outlet while he ate.

With a plan in place, he contacted Tyler on Xbox to make sure there was no trip in store for the Creasy family. Since school was in session, he was fairly certain there wouldn't be. After a quick conversation to get some information without actually asking for it, he was able to find that the Creasy family had no intention of making any travels or excursions over the next few weeks. The next step was to get approval for vacation from work.

With the FBI, a short-notice vacation was normally a little difficult, as scheduled time off usually required three to four weeks' notice in any situations not involving a family death. However, dealing with the issues they saw on a daily basis allowed for members of the Cyber Crimes Division to "take a break" from it all to "get their heads right." Brian hadn't needed a break, as he was able to separate his feelings from what he saw, but he had taken a few along the way so he didn't stand out. The last "break" he "needed to take" was about nine months ago. This break was a little early for him but shouldn't draw suspicion. He went to his boss the next day and requested two weeks' vacation starting Monday. Without question, it was granted.

Chapter 3
A Gruesome Discovery

Tyler was absent from school and the calls home went unanswered. Similarly, Eric was absent from work and didn't bother to call in. As a result, the local police department was called to check in on the family. This was one of the "perks" of living in a small town. When the school calls home and the parents' job to check on one of the few students not at school and their calls go unanswered, the police check up on the family.

Deputy Childress volunteered to take the call. He enjoyed the ride out to the country roads and this was one he hadn't been down in some time. The Creasy house was one on the better side of town and few calls came in to the department for that area. Like they say, "the squeaky wheel gets the grease" and this wheel didn't squeak.

On these rides, this country boy loved to listen to old school rap. Here was this "corn fed" six-foot-three, two-hundred-and-thirty-pound horse-breaking, steer-wrestling "Cowboy" listening to the Sugar Hill Gang and rapping every lyric of all three M.C.s from Wonder Mike's opening to Hank's "after school, I take a dip in the pool, which is really off the wall" and on to Master Gee's "I'm gonna freak ya here, I'm gonna freak you there, I'm gonna freak you right outta this atmosphere" and everything in between. This wasn't the radio edit; the full extended version was what this country boy enjoyed.

When Deputy Childress arrived, the song was fading out. *Perfect timing*, he thought. But it didn't take long for him to sense that something was wrong. As he made his way down the long, winding driveway, things seemed eerily quiet, although peaceful. Upon his arrival at the house, it didn't take long for him to notice the smoke-marred siding surrounding an upstairs window. He went to the front door and knocked. When his knocks went unanswered, he grabbed the door handle, which was unlocked, and opened the door. He called out, but no one answered. He was immediately aware of an odd, sweet smell that he didn't recognize. As he climbed the stairs and headed toward the source of the smoke, the smell grew stronger and, when he arrived at the master bedroom door, it was quite apparent that the source of the smell was that of burnt flesh. He held back the vomit that was trying to vacate his stomach and quickly made his way down the stairs. He nearly stumbled when the stairs made a 90-degree turn toward the front door. Thankfully, the railing was sturdy and was able to support him as he slammed into it. He barely made it out the front door to the lawn before he could hold it no longer. Then, the roast beef sandwich he had eaten for lunch, along with the sea salt and pepper chips and his traditional "cheat" treat of one Twix Bar, erupted onto the pristine lawn. When he regained his composure, he went back to his police cruiser and took a swig of his Wild Cherry Pepsi, swished it around in his mouth, and spat it onto the driveway. He followed with a full swig to wash the vomit taste out of his mouth. Then he called his boss, Chief Christopher Caldwell.

Chief Chris Caldwell had over twenty years of experience on the job in this small town and, by now, thought he had seen everything. Being an African American Chief of Police in a small southern town led to many interesting days. He had a number of people resist arrest by saying, "No black man is going to take me to jail," but this black man always made it happen. Sometimes, they went more easily than their boasts. Other times, it was a little more difficult, but they always went to jail, either the hard way or the easy way. It made no difference to "The Chief." He almost enjoyed "busting heads" of racist resistors, but he also liked it when everything went smoothly and no one got hurt.

Chief Caldwell's appearance put one in the mind of Charles Barkley, bald head included. He wasn't a spitting image of the Hall of Famer, but looked like he could be a half-brother or cousin and he had one close friend that constantly reminded him of his look-a-like by continually calling him "Chuck." Chris was a former high school star athlete that excelled in football, baseball, and basketball. He dabbled in boxing, which was the sport he'd always loved, but he never made a serious run at it. The other sports afforded him college scholarship opportunities, whereas boxing didn't. He ended up going to Grambling State University on a football scholarship and he played both football and baseball while majoring in Criminal Justice.

Chris had a plan. If neither of the sports worked out, he'd become a cop and he'd be a fair one. He'd ask questions and shoot later. He knew that, within his community, he might be deemed a "sell out," but he also knew the best way to change a system or to ensure that police powers weren't abused was to be the policeman with the power. That way, he could change the behavior from within. He also knew that he couldn't change police behavior everywhere but he could in his hometown. A shoulder injury put a damper on his baseball dreams and he just wasn't NFL material. Therefore, football didn't take him any further than college. Although he was greatly disappointed in the back of his mind, he could hear his single father telling him "everything happens for a reason." Perhaps not making it to the next level was saving him from CTE or another serious injury or maybe not making it to the next level would mean a different blessing was in his future.

It didn't take long for him to realize the reason for not making it to the professional level in sports. That reason was a pretty young lady who arrived in his hometown not long after he joined the force.

Luckily, he pulled her over for speeding. She was late to her job as a paralegal at a law firm, and he was parked along a normal speeding corridor. Once he walked up to the car, he couldn't untie his tongue. She just smiled and chuckled. Instead of giving her a ticket, he violated every protocol of being a police officer and simply wrote his phone number on a piece of paper and handed it to her. When he was finally able to speak, he said "Have a good day, ma'am." He had never attempted that feat before and never repeated it after that day. He didn't have to. Tina Hughes called him a few days later and they met for coffee. This time, he was able to untie his tongue. As a result, Chris Caldwell became a man who was happily married to the former Tina Hughes. Together, they had two children who were now adults. His oldest child was his twin. When his son was young, he referred to him as "Mini-Me." He followed in his footsteps into law enforcement and was an agent for the Naval Criminal Investigative Service, better known as NCIS. His daughter looked like her mother but was even more beautiful. She followed in her mother's footsteps and entered law from a different angle. She was a lawyer at a Memphis law firm.

Even though Chief Caldwell had seen bizarre, crazy and, more often than he liked, terrible things, this was like nothing he'd ever seen before. The house was spared, but the upstairs portion was greatly damaged. In the center of this "hell" were the severely burnt remains of a man sitting in a chair and a woman tied to the ceiling and floor.

In questioning the neighbors, Chief Caldwell's team was not able to find out much about the Creasy family other than the family consisted of a couple and what most believed was their thirteen-year-old son. They were extremely secretive and some believed they sold drugs. Also, many thought they were some sort of foster parents, as there were a number of children, both boys and girls, that visited the home frequently. Usually, there would be one or two in addition to the teenaged boy for a week or more at a time, and then, they'd be gone. But, the one boy, presumably their son, always remained. In examining the damage to the home, they were unable to find the remains of any children. That both scared Chris and showed promise. The scary questions were "what happened to the child?" and "where is he?" The promise came from no evidence of children being killed in this gruesome scene. That showed hope of the boy still being alive.

After getting a description of the young teen and contacting the middle school to find out the boy's name, Chief Caldwell contacted headquarters and put out an Amber Alert on young Tyler Creasy and reported the apparent kidnapping to the FBI. He ensured the bodies went to the county morgue and contacted the County Coroner to do a full autopsy on the remains. There was no question as to whether or not this was an accident or murder, but he needed to know how and why they were killed and, most importantly, who killed these two people because that, hopefully, would lead to the boy.

While they were waiting for the FBI, Chief Caldwell set out to find out what he could about Eric and the family. He left Officer Childress and Officer Hughes in charge of looking for clues at the house. His first stop was the auto parts store where Eric Creasy worked. By the time Chris arrived, everyone in the store knew Eric Creasy was dead. In a small town like this with social media and a stable gossip line, news travelled fast. When Chris talked to the manager, some things didn't add up. At the store, Eric made fifteen dollars an hour. By the look of his house and land, there was no way he'd be able to afford that property on what he earned at the store. That, along with the fact that Tammy was a homemaker with no apparent income, made the mortgage nearly impossible to pay.

A trip to the school was next. Chris talked to all of Tyler's teachers. Without exception, they told him that Tyler was bright, always did his homework, made good grades, stayed out of trouble, but stayed to himself with the exception of his two close friends, Lashaun Butler and Jackson Holmes. Outside of those two individuals, Tyler didn't associate with anyone at school.

Chris contacted the parents of the two boys and arranged for interviews with the children. He hoped the boys could provide some insight into the home life of Tyler and the Creasy Family.

Lashaun's house was first. He was a quiet kid; polite and bright. After three minutes in the home, anyone could tell that his parents, Calvin and Rachel, were loving, and Lashaun and his brother and sisters were happy children. In speaking with Lashuan, Chris was able to find out that Tyler was a secretive kid. Lashaun had never been to Tyler's house and Tyler was rarely seen away from school or the soccer field and never without one or both of his parents. Lashaun said he thought Tyler's parents were "like those people he saw on TV with bunkers and lots of canned food."

"You mean survivalists," injected Calvin.

"Yes, sir, survivalists," answered Lashaun. "And... never mind."

"And what, son?"

"I think Mr. Eric sold drugs."

"What makes you say that?" asked Chris.

"Well, every time we have one of those 'say no to drugs' assemblies, Tyler says that he'd be homeless if everyone said no to drugs. At first, I thought he was joking, but he always says it and other things. You see, Tyler is very sarcastic and funny. Sometimes, he says things and people don't know if he's joking or serious and Jackson and I crack up. He is one of my best friends and just when I think I have him figured out, he says something that, even for me, it's hard to tell if he's serious or not, but it's funny. But he says, 'I can get you some weed if you want it,' and I don't know if he's kidding around or if he's serious."

"The neighbors said there were other kids at his house sometimes. Do you know who they are or do they go to school with you?" Chris inquired.

"No, I never saw them and they never come to school and Tyler doesn't really talk about them, other than joke around and say that his parents got him a new girlfriend. And, sometimes, he'd say that his mom got a new boyfriend. I don't know what he meant by that, but I never met any other kids that lived in his house."

"Thank you, son. You have been a big help," Chris stated. "Let me know if you need anything or if you think of anything else."

"Mr. Caldwell, are you going to find my friend?" he asked.

"I sure hope so, Lashaun... I sure hope so. Mr. and Mrs. Butler, I thank you for allowing me to speak to the fine young man. It is easy to tell that you guys have done a terrific job raising him. Please call me if I can help you with anything regarding this matter or anything else." After he exchanged pleasantries and gave his card to both parents, Chris left and went back to the office.

This thing about the other children really had Chris' mind wondering. He intended to call family services to see if the Creasys were foster parents. But first, he would meet with Jackson Holmes and his family as arranged at six that evening.

While en route to his office, Chris received a call over the radio from Deputy Trenton Childress.

"Chief, you need to come to the house. There is a lot here to show you."

"I'm on my way." Chris didn't need to ask Trent the specifics. He had come to know and respect him over the six years they worked with and around each other. As a result of their working together in the past, he knew that Trent would not discuss case specifics over the radio and, if Trent said he needed to be there, he needed to be there.

Once there, Trent took Chris out to the barn in the back of the property. There, he saw over one hundred potted marijuana plants and a large number of plants in a separate section hanging from the rafters drying out.

"Holy shit!" exclaimed Chris. "There's gotta be over a hundred thousand dollars' worth of weed in here."

"What do you think, Chris? Was this a drug deal gone wrong?"

"I don't know. If this was a drug deal, wouldn't they take this stuff?" replied Chris.

"There's more in the house," stated Trent.

"More marijuana?"

"No, there's more I need to show you. You need to see what's in the basement," Trent replied.

Trent took Chris to the basement of the house. There, he was shown a room in the back corner of the basement. This room had a bed, a large array of sexual paraphernalia, and a bunch of camera equipment.

"What were these people into?" asked Chris.

Trent went to a cabinet in the corner of the room and showed Chris volumes upon volumes of DVDs neatly arranged and labeled.

"Have you looked at them?" asked Chris.

"No, but Reggie took a few back to the office to

screen. I'm waiting on a call from him to let me know what's on them. He should be calling any minute."

***

As he drove down the road, Officer Hughes heard the words, "You're as smooth as Tennessee Whiskey, you're as sweet as strawberry wine" play on his radio. He couldn't help but join in. "You're as warm as a glass of brandy and, honey, I stay stoned on your love all the time." The good thing about Officer Hughes singing in his police SUV was that the windows were rolled up and no one could be harmed by the horrible singing that started deep within his chest, came up through his untrained vocal chords, and emitted from his mouth. Even his own mother said that his singing was reminiscent of coyotes howling. Still, Officer Hughes loved the song. He had a friend that swore up and down that the song was not about a woman, as most believed, but it was about marijuana. "It's the country version of *Brown Sugar* by D'Angelo," he would say.

None of that mattered to Officer Hughes. He liked good music regardless of genre and this young African American man was singing one of his favorite country songs. And that might soon be followed by a Motown classic or one of the latest rap hits.

Officer Reggie Hughes was relatively new on the force. He was a distant cousin of Tina and, thus, Chris—which wasn't unusual because, in this town, everyone was a distant cousin of someone else. He loved his job and was excited about making a difference. He was a young man that always had a smile on his face and the smile seemed to get brighter when he put on his uniform. Reggie was not a big man. He was about 5'9" tall and 170 pounds soaking wet, but he was no pushover. He would not stand for a man to put his hands on a woman, any sort of child abuse or neglect, or anything to do with drugs and children. These fundamental beliefs came from his life experiences and upbringing he received from his single mother and his "other family."

The "other family" was a couple with two children, the oldest of which, Omar, was his best friend. "Pops," as he referred to the father, always stressed how to treat a woman and that a MAN never put his hands on a woman, NEVER. The protection of children was what he learned at home by helping to raise his baby brother, who was thirteen years his junior. The drug part was because of what he saw drugs do to his older brother.

His older brother was a gifted athlete and a star in basketball, baseball, and football. In one football game, he was likely to play quarterback, receiver, defensive back, and even the kicker/punter. All that went away after drugs, both using and selling, became more of a priority in his life than anything else. Reggie also saw what drugs did to other children and teenagers that grew up with him. He saw them as a plague upon his community and would do anything and everything within his power to get rid of them. But there was one incident that made Officer Hughes decide that he wanted to be a "cop."

***

Reggie and Omar were riding down the road with Omar driving. They both had some marijuana with them, as most teenagers and those in their early twenties did. Omar, distracted by their conversation about some young lady they were interested in, ran a stop sign. Thankfully, there was no traffic from the crossing direction, but there was a police officer that witnessed the whole thing. This officer immediately pulled them over. Two black men in a nice car carrying weed could have been a recipe for disaster. As the officer approached the vehicle, the two young men went through all of the training that "Pops" had given them. Be respectful, hands in plain sight, and no sudden movements. "Most of all, BE RESPECTFUL regardless of what happens, what he says or does, you make it home. I'll deal with any bullshit if need be," he would say. As if they had been training together for this moment like a dance routine, their movements seemed synchronized as Reggie grabbed his wallet from his back pocket and placed it and his hands on the dash and Omar put his on the steering wheel.

"Your license and registration, please," requested the officer.

"Sir, they are on the back side of my sun visor. May I retrieve them?" This location was a Pops must.

"Go ahead."

Omar deliberately but not quickly reached up and folded down the visor to retrieve the documents and handed them to the officer. As he did, he made sure the officer saw his military dependent identification card. This was another "Pops" lesson. The military ID in a military town couldn't hurt, especially if the officer was a veteran.

"Do you know why I pulled you over?"

"Honestly, no, I don't. I know I wasn't speeding."

"You ran a stop sign back there."

"Did I? Officer, that was not my intent; my brother and I were just talking about this girl and I must have been wrapped up in that conversation."

"Yes, you did. Do you have any warrants?"

"No, sir. None that I know of."

"How about you?" the officer addressed Reggie.

"No, sir. I had some outstanding tickets, but I took care of them last month."

"If you give me your ID," the officer was speaking directly to Reggie, "and you guys come back clean, you can be on your way."

Reggie opened his wallet and handed his license to the officer.

The officer took the IDs and headed to his cruiser.

"Bro, what about the weed, though?" Omar asked.

"If he doesn't search, we're good."

After a few minutes, the officer returned. "It looks like you guys are good. Reggie, you were telling the truth. Dude, you need to slow down. Your speeding fines are getting expensive and don't forget about the last one. Your court date is next week unless you pay the fine."

"Yes sir, my bank account is feeling it. My insurance too. Thanks for the reminder."

"Now, I must be honest with you guys. I can smell it. How much do you have?"

Omar and Reggie looked at one another and Omar nodded to Reggie and Reggie nodded back.

"Officer…" Omar paused and looked at the name tag. "Officer Jennings, honestly, we each have one joint that we were planning to smoke at a party."

"You two young men have been nothing but honest and respectful with me, and Reggie, you didn't have to give me your license and you guys didn't have to fess up to the weed. Because of this, I am sending you on your way with this warning. Pay more attention to the road. Running that stop sign could've gotten someone killed. And keep that weed at home. You two young men have a good night and I hope things with that young lady worked out for one of you. Omar, tell your dad 'thanks for his service.'" With that, Officer Jennings handed Omar all the documents, turned, and walked away.

As Omar pulled off, Reggie quipped, "Illuminati!! Your ass is definitely in the Illuminati. How many times is this? Five?"

Reggie's comment was based on the fact that Omar was constantly doing little stuff like speeding, running a stop sign, getting caught making out with a girl in a parking lot, or carrying small amounts of weed, and he never got so much as a ticket. This convinced all of Omar's friends, including Reggie, that he was in the Illuminati.

"I just figured it out," Reggie said with excitement.

"Figured what out?" questioned Omar.

"What I want to do. I am going to be a cop so I can be a cop like that guy. No harassment, no unnecessary arrests, no tickets. That's what I'm going to be. A cop that protects and serves, not harasses and arrests." A year and a half later, Reggie took the oath to protect and serve.

* * *

Officer Hughes arrived back at the station. As he walked in, he greeted Pearl, the station receptionist.

"Good afternoon, Pearl."

"Good afternoon, Reggie."

"How are you today?" he asked.

"Fine."

"I didn't ask how you looked. I asked how you are feeling," he replied with a grin.

Pearl blushed and laughed.

This was part of the everyday playful flirting between this young man and a happily married older woman. There was no harassment or intention of action. It was just a young man trying to help make a lady feel good about herself.

Reggie headed to his office, put a DVD in his computer, and hit play. After about thirty seconds of watching it, he started to cry. He couldn't believe what was starting to unfold in front of his eyes. A minute in, he was sobbing like a baby and couldn't hold down his lunch. He grabbed the trashcan next to his desk and let the hot wings from Shane's Shack go. He couldn't take anymore. He stopped the DVD, went to the one-stall men's bathroom, locked the door, and sat there and cried for about five minutes before he got himself together. He splashed some water on his face, wiped off with a towel, went to his desk, and called the chief.

"What's up, Reg?" asked Chris as he answered the phone.

"Chief, this is some sick stuff. That poor kid. Chief... His... D.," the word "dad" wouldn't come out of his mouth. A DAD or FATHER didn't do that to his child. "Chief, that sick son of a bitch was screwing his own kid."

"Reggie, what are you saying?" He couldn't believe what Officer Hughes was telling him. This was his town. Chief Caldwell knew pretty much everyone and everything that happened in his town. How could something like this be happening "on his watch?" He needed clarification. Was this Officer Hughes using slang or was he being literal? "Officer Hughes, what exactly are you telling me?"

"Chief, that man was having sex with his son and someone was recording it. I only looked at the first minute or so of one video. But there was a man lying on a bed with a boy before the act and the boy called him 'Dad.' Chief, once it started, I had to stop. I couldn't watch anymore."

"Okay, Reggie. We'll sort this out later. I'll be there in about thirty minutes or so."

"Was that Reggie? What's up, Chief?" asked Trenton.

"Trent, Reggie says the man was sexually abusing his kid. It's all right there on video."

"Boss, most of these videos have different names on them. Only the first ten had the name Tyler on them."

"Yeah, Trent, I saw that. I am afraid that we may have a child pornography ring here. We'll need to call in the feds on this one also. Reggie was right."

"Right about what?" Trent asked.

"That Eric Creasy was a sick son of a bitch! And, if what Reggie is telling me is true and all these DVDs are the same, I think he may have gotten what he deserved."

Chapter 4
The Stakeout

Brian knew he needed an inconspicuous vehicle capable of holding a bunch of equipment that would be comfortable enough to spend hours at a time inside.

An RV! That'd do the trick, he thought to himself, but he almost blurted out loud.

He was able to find a used RV on Craig's List. It was one of those RVs that looked like an overgrown passenger van. It wasn't in great condition, but it ran well and all of the essentials were in place. It needed a good cleaning and several of the cabinet doors were broken off. The inside had a musty smell. Obviously, the RV had a leak somewhere and having just sat in place with a leak caused some mold and mildew to form. Once Brian took a closer look, he was able to find a leak where the roof met a sidewall just above the bathroom. The fix would be simple, but the removal of the mold would be a bit more difficult. Still, the price was right at $3,000 for an RV this size with a well-running 7.3L Ford Power Stroke diesel engine. He paid for the vehicle in cash and registered it under one of his aliases.

A few hours in the bathroom allowed him to remove the wall in front of the leak, use bleach, followed by an essential oil cleaner called "Thieves Spray" to remove the mold and to make the area somewhat cosmetically sound. The next evening, he spent another few hours installing an additional alternator, dedicated to a separate group of batteries, that would be used to power command central. Then he installed his monitors, motorcycle-docking station, and communication equipment. All said and done, he had a very nice mobile command center. It wasn't cosmetically desirable, but it was well equipped.

Brian headed south from Quantico, Virginia to Tennessee. The trip was uneventful and he made the journey in good time. Once in the Memphis area, he found his way to the RV park he had scouted out online. He hooked up his RV and made preparations for the days to come. He was pretty tired from the trip. There would be no stalking of his prey tonight. However, he would make a dry run to the location to make sure he knew the route and that there were no surprises along the way.

Once he made it to the house, he slowed his motorcycle enough to take in as much as he could without looking suspicious. Once he realized the coast was clear and no traffic as coming either way, he pulled his motorcycle to the side of the road, hopped off, and pretended to act like he was making adjustments to the motor. In reality, he was looking for cameras or anything else that would make his actual stalking more difficult. There didn't appear to be any near the property. He climbed back on the bike and headed back toward the RV. On the way back, he stopped to get a bite to eat. Once back at "Command Central," he plugged the motorcycle in to charge, made plans to see some of the sights, take pictures while there, and post them on social media websites to support his "vacation." Day one would involve a trip to Graceland (he'd always wanted to see Elvis' manor anyway). He fell asleep around 11:30 that evening and didn't bother to set an alarm.

He awoke the next morning around eight, which was way later than his usual 5:30 wake time, but the trip had exhausted him. He brushed his teeth and threw on his running shorts, t-shirt, and shoes. He put his Bluetooth headphones in his ears and put his phone in his armband running sleeve, but not before he selected shuffle on his workout playlist. He started out on his run. He always ran against the traffic when running on roads. He didn't trust drivers. There were just many times that he saw drivers looking down at their phones as they veered a foot or two either to the right and across the lane dividing line or, more importantly to joggers and bikers, a foot or two to the left onto the shoulder or into the bike lane.

The first song he heard on the playlist was "Bombs

Over Baghdad" by Outkast. He loved that song, as the driving beat would not allow a slow running tempo, but he generally preferred to hear that song at the end of a run. He was afraid running at that tempo this early would use too much of his energy too early. Five miles later, he finished his run in above average time.

I guess an Outkast start didn't hurt much, he thought.

He climbed the steps of the RV, grabbed some water and, after he cooled off, he took a shower and headed off to Graceland.

When he arrived at Graceland, he was struck at how small the house felt on the inside. Standing outside, he could see the manor was massive at over 17,000 square feet, but still, the inside felt smaller. Maybe that was because the tour didn't allow access to the upstairs. He heard a teenage kid on the tour quip, "We can't go up there because that's where Elvis lives and is watching us as he rakes in the cash." This caused Brian to chuckle, partly because it was funny and partly because he shared a similar thought. After his tour of Graceland, he went on to tour Elvis' airplane, the *Lisa Marie*. In all, it was more than he expected. While he was there, he made sure to take a few selfies and posted them on his social media pages to give the appearance of his vacation.

He returned to the RV, trying to avoid any conversation amounting to anything more than a casual "Hello" to the other residents at the RV park. He didn't want to get roped into a southern hospitality dinner, a long conversation, or someone casually stopping by while he was out. He let his motorcycle charge for a number of hours while he recharged his own batteries by taking a nap. He set his alarm for 10 p.m. He awoke, grabbed his "bag of tricks," and headed out to the Creasy residence. He was careful to arrive at the Creasy property with no traffic in front or behind him. Once next to the property, he turned in to the woods and pushed his motorcycle off the road quickly. He found a corner to lay the bike down and covered it up with some camouflage netting. Then he found a good spot to make his blind to set up his equipment. There, he set up his remote-controlled telescope and trained it on the house.

He sat and waited for all the lights to go out. Once they were out, he waited another hour or so. It was quiet. Looking up, he saw more stars than he was able to see in the lightly-polluted Northern Virginia. All of this was peaceful. From time to time, he was startled by a rabbit running through leaves, the occasional hoot of an owl, and the rare passing vehicle. The thought occurred to him that this was ... "heavenly." But that thought was fleeting. He had a mission to accomplish and "heavenly" was the farthest from what this mission would be for him or his target.

When he was fairly certain all were asleep, he made his move. A quick tour of the entire property was first. On the tour, he found an outbuilding near the back edge of the property. The building contained a large amount of marijuana. This must have been how Eric paid for this property and his enterprises. The drugs would surely help with Brian's cover. The soon-to-be deaths of Eric and Tammy Creasy could be blamed on a drug deal gone wrong.

Next would be the trickiest part of the night. He moved swiftly and quietly to the house. Once there, he attached his miniature microphones to the main room window, the kitchen window, and what appeared to be a basement window. In the same locations, he placed small cameras. These cameras and microphones were able to link up to the small transmitter he planted in a nearby tree. That transmitter sent data from the house cameras and the telescope via a UHF signal that he could receive back at his RV This kept everything off the Cyber Crimes grid. Tapping into the Creasys' Wi-Fi would have been easier; however, Brian couldn't ensure whatever was going on in that house wouldn't be picked up by his own people at the FBI over the internet if he did.

After successfully installing his equipment, Brian headed back to Command Central, otherwise known as the RV. The ride back was oddly peaceful. The night was quiet, the air was clean, the temperature was perfect, but the future was... the future was going to be Hell. Once at the RV, he did an operational test of the equipment. The telescope was working, the cameras were all up and running, but the kitchen microphone didn't appear to be operating, or it was dead quiet in there. He set up the system to record everything and went to bed. When he arose the next morning, he went for his run. Once back at the RV, he reviewed his recordings. Nothing seemed out of the ordinary until Tyler was about to head off to school.

"Tyler," a man's voice said, "are you looking forward to seeing your girlfriend again this evening?"

Tyler's response was a hesitant and shaky "Yes."

His girlfriend? Why does this man sound more excited than Tyler?

Brian headed off to the Civil Rights museum. When he saw where Martin Luther King was assassinated, he forgot about his "mission." He couldn't separate his emotions from the situation. His training didn't prepare him for the emotions he was feeling here. The hatred, the dread, and the wondering what would have happened had the events of that day not occurred all overpowered his training. While he was there, he took the obligatory pictures and posted them on the internet. All the while, he couldn't escape wondering what this country would be like had this great man not been cut down in his prime by James Earl Ray's bullet.

He headed back to the RV. On the way, he grabbed a bite to eat. Once back, he sat and ate and reviewed the feeds from the day. Tyler went off to school and the Creasy adults stayed at home. Eric Creasy seemed anxious and even excited. He kept telling his wife Tammy, "Tonight is going to be incredible. Racquel is always special. She kind of reminds me of a young version of you. Tyler should be very happy."

Brian's thoughts about what was in store for the evening raced from the innocent to the perverse. That night, as he watched from afar via his equipment, perverse wasn't even close to what he saw and heard. Brian looked in periodically. It was like a bad car wreck. He wanted to turn away and he did, but he had to know how bad this was. The sickness that he witnessed was watched by ten men and women in the room.

As the two children entered the room, a man's voice from a couch said, "Okay, let's get this party started, man," except that "man" was pronounced oddly. His version of the word had two syllables and sounded more like "may-yen." He sounded extremely excited about the events that were to unfold.

When the children were done, the adults took turns with the children, some with Tyler, others with that poor girl. One of the men appeared to be the girl's father. Then, there was the "may-yen" guy. He said, "I want that young buck first and then that filly, may-yen." Brian couldn't shut down the emotions. It was too hard. Shutting down the emotions couldn't be done with the video on. Finally, he turned it off. He sat and sobbed. Sorrow, anger, hatred, regret, remorse… all of the old feelings were coming back. He knew that Tyler would be the one that would allow Brian get "into the black."

The bad news was that Tyler and this unlucky young girl that someone called "Racquel" were exploited. And even worse, it appeared from the children's behavior that it wasn't the first time for either of them. The poor girl couldn't have been more than twelve years old. The good news was that this was the last night anyone would have to suffer at the hands of Eric Creasy.

Chapter 5
The Investigation Continues

The Holmes family was delayed a bit, but Chief Caldwell was able to meet with them that evening. Chris made his greetings to the family and took an extra minute with his longtime friend, Moses Holmes. Then the three of them sat down in the family's study.

"Jackson, what can you tell me about Tyler?" he asked.

"Well…" Jackson was hesitant and afraid. That didn't take a policeman to detect.

"Son, I am trying to help. If there is anything you can tell me about Tyler, anything at all, it might help me find him. I don't want him to be hurt."

"He won't be hurt anymore?"

"No, he won't…wait, anymore? Was he being hurt?"

"Officer Caldwell, he told me that if I ever told anyone, they would kill him."

"Who would kill him?"

"His p-p-parents!"

"Jackson, Tyler's parents are gone. They can't kill him. If someone else can hurt him, then I need to find that person to stop it. What do you know, son?" he asked compassionately.

"They made him do things. Things with other kids, sometimes other boys or girls, sometimes with men or women, even his mom and dad."

"Jackson, why didn't you tell me?" his father interjected.

"Jackson, it's all right," assured the chief.

At this point, Chief Caldwell didn't want to come between a father and son, but he knew this young man was in a very difficult dilemma. He gave Moses a look that expressed his understanding of the man's disappointment, but this was not the time to berate him. Instinctively, he knew that this bit of conversation called for an informal and sympathetic tone.

"Moses, he couldn't. He was afraid for Tyler. I understand. He didn't want Tyler killed." Chief Caldwell saw an opening to let Jackson know that he was his ally. "Jackson, did he mention any names? Is there anyone I can talk to about this?" he continued.

"No, he never mentioned any names. I'm pretty sure he never knew any. Except this one girl that he said he really liked. He said she wasn't like all the rest. He said the others were like zombies but 'Rocky' was really nice. When they were alone together, not doing the stuff they did, they talked about getting out of the craziness and having a normal life. 'Rocky' was kind of his girlfriend. But not a girlfriend; more of a girl...friend." Jackson was sure to install a long pause in between the two words to illustrate the meaning.

"Do you know her last name or if he talked to her online or anything?"

"He said he played *Call of Duty* with her on Xbox. They both had to sneak online. She was one of his Xbox friends."

"Do you know her Xbox gamertag?"

"No, I don't. He promised not to tell anyone or to let anyone become her friend other than him. He said that she was terrified of her parents and they promised to kill her if their stuff ever got out."

"Jackson, you've been a very big help. More than you will ever know. Is there anything else you can tell me?"

"No, Chief Caldwell. Please, find my friend."

"I'll do everything that I can. We are going to try our hardest and I can promise you this… I won't stop until I find Tyler."

Chief Caldwell walked to the front door and Jackson's father followed. He signaled for Mr. Holmes to come outside with them.

"Moses, I know you are mad or maybe disappointed. Go easy on him. This isn't his fault and he didn't do anything wrong. There is no telling what would have happened if he had said anything. From what I have seen, these people were very sick and killing that little boy wasn't out of the question. Jackson is going through a difficult time right now and he needs your support and nothing else. I have the FBI in on this and we will do everything we can to find Tyler."

"I hear you, Chris. It's scary what goes on around us and we have no clue. Good luck in finding that boy. Let me know if there is anything else we can do to help."

"I will, brother. I'll talk to you later. God bless."

"God bless you too."

Chris got on the phone right away and called Deputy Childress, who was keeping watch at the Creasy house.

"Trenton, find that boy's Xbox. We need to look at his friends."

"Will do, Chief. I'm on it. I'll call you when I have it."

Trenton searched the house from the basement to the attic and found no Xbox. When he looked in greater detail, he found Xbox power and video connection cables on the television in what appeared to be the boy's bedroom, but there was no Xbox there. He jumped on the phone.

"Chief, it's gone."

"Come again, Trent?"

"The Xbox. It's gone. The connections are there, but someone took the dern thing."

"That's not good ... but it's our first lead."

"Chief, how can something not there be a lead?"

"Trent, it's a lead because someone took it. There is a reason they took it. Now we need to figure out why."

"That's why you're the chief!"

"That and my astonishing good looks," he said lightheartedly.

"And your humble personality," Trent replied.

By the time he was wrapped up at the crime scene, it was late. The schools and auto-parts store where Eric worked were closed. Further investigation would have to wait until the morning. He didn't like to wait. He knew he was in for a night of little sleep because he would be worrying about that young teen until he found him. And that wouldn't start until the morning. For now, he knew he had missed dinner, so he would grab some food on the go. He made a call to Tina.

"Hey, love, I'm finally heading home. I'm going to grab something to eat. Do you want anything?"

"Just you to make it here safely… and perhaps a sweet treat."

"Okay. I'll see you soon. I love you."

"More!" Tina's standard reply.

Chris jumped into the SUV and started it up. The radio started playing that unmistakable baseline from the Temptations "Papa Was a Rolling Stone." He realized the strings hadn't started yet. That meant the song had just started. This song always made the hairs on the back of his neck stand up. The grit, the honesty, the four-minute instrumental lead-in on the full-length version, the harmonies, the hand claps, and on and on all led to what Chris referred to as a musical experience in one song. If it was on, he couldn't turn it off, and if he arrived at his destination before it was over, he would sit and listen until the very end, if circumstances permitted. He couldn't help but be the "sixth Temp" that sang all of the parts. He listened and sang along with the song on his way to the local diner. He even called in his order to the diner with the song playing the background.

"Jimmy's Diner. How can I help you?"

Chief Caldwell turned down the radio, but he could clearly hear, "Mama hung her head and said, son, Papa was a rolling stone, wherever he laid his hat was his home."

"Treena, is that you?"

"And when he died," the harmonies continued until the unmistakable pain and anger in Dennis Edwards' voice cried out, "all he left us was alone."

"Chief, you know it is. What can I get you? The usual?"

"Yes, ma'am."

"With or without the two slices of apple pie?

"With."

"One plain cheeseburger – medium rare – fries, two slices of apple pie, and a cherry coke. It'll be ready in about ten minutes."

"Thanks, Treena. See ya soon."

When he got to the diner four minutes later, he knew his food was nowhere near being done. So he sat and listened while he waited. When the song ended, he went inside.

"Hey, Chief. I have your order right here. That'll be—"

Chief Caldwell interrupted, "Treena, we do this all the time. You're going to tell me that the total is seven forty-six and I'm going to give you a ten-dollar bill and tell you to keep the change."

Treena smiled as Chris gave her the ten-dollar bill.

"You have a good night, Treena. Forty-five minutes until you're off, right?"

"You know it. You have a good night and a safe ride home. Tell Tina that Treena said 'hello'."

"I will, Treena. Bye now."

Chris headed out the door, jumped into his SUV, and headed home. There was solace in knowing that he'd be home with Tina, but he knew he was in for a long night of restless sleep, if any.

When he arrived, he was greeted by Tina standing in the door. This was out of the norm for them, but she knew that today was one of those especially rough ones.

"I see you went to see Treena," she remarked while pointing at the to-go box in his hand.

"Treena said to tell Tina hello," he replied.

As soon as he was close enough, Tina wrapped her arms around the man she proclaimed to be "The Love Her Life." He hugged back. The ills of the world seemed to drift away if but for a brief moment. He kissed her lips, then her forehead, as he was his custom, and asked, "How was your day?"

"Mine was fine, but I hear you had a rough one."

"I did, and I don't think it is going to get any better anytime soon, but let's not talk about that. What's on TV?"

They moved to the couch and turned on something unimportant to watch while Chris ate his meal and they ate the slices of pie together. When they were done, they made the journey to bed, and Chris, as predicted, tossed and turned all night.

When Chris made it out of bed in the morning, showered, and headed downstairs, Tina was there to greet him with a freshly cooked breakfast. This was another abnormal situation.

"Somebody is awake. Good morning, love."

"Awake isn't really what I'd call it. Finally up out of bed more like it." He continued, "To be awake would imply that I was asleep or am not asleep. I'm not sure which I am right now."

"You sound like this is what you need." Tina handed him a cup of coffee.

Chris took the coffee and placed it on the counter, stepped toward Tina, and embraced her in his arms. She hugged him back. "This is what I need." Again, all the ills of the world vanished for that moment. He released his embrace, grabbed his coffee, and sat down and ate his breakfast. When he was done, he gave Tina another hug, kissed her lips and her forehead, and headed out to start his day.

Chapter 6
A Terrible Past

The next morning, Brian woke up and found it hard to get out of bed. He felt a sort of depression. It was all coming back to him. He had trained for years to not let this happen. But the video showed him things too familiar. He had to pull it together. After lying in bed for ten minutes, he forced himself to take charge of the day. Tyler would not be freed if he didn't act. He got out of bed and went for his run. *A run will help me get my head on straight*, he thought.

He got himself dressed and started out on his run. The run did anything but clear his head. All he could think about was his past.

His mind flashed back to his childhood. The images of good times. Good times like going to the movies with his father, mother and "Uncle Cody." He enjoyed movies. They were his escape from the real world. Some of his favorites were *Finding Nemo, Lion King, Shrek, and Monsters Inc.* All of his favorites had happy endings; an ending he thought he'd never see.

The images of bad times also plagued him on his run. Bad times, like his father forcing him to watch as his mother, father, and "Uncle Cody" engaged in sex. Worse times, when each of them took turns with him. Praying to God to make it stop because it didn't feel right. It didn't feel right because he was sworn to secrecy and the threats that "Uncle Cody" would kill his mother, Sydney. The look of fear in his mother's eyes as all of this took place told Brian all he needed to know. She didn't want to be here; Sydney didn't want any of this to happen and she was very afraid.

For years, these acts went on. From the age of nine into his teens. Brian saw no hope. He resigned himself to a life of violation, shame, and sadness. Then one day, it all came to an end.

A few months after his thirteenth birthday, when he was feeling particularly down, one of his teachers brought him to the side and asked him, "What's going on? You aren't acting like your normal self. Your grades are slipping and you all of a sudden have an attitude."

Brian used his normal cover of "Coach Horton, I'm sorry. Things aren't going great at home. My parents are fighting and I think they may be getting a divorce. I'll be all right."

He could see in Coach's eyes that he didn't buy his excuse like everyone else did, and Coach's phone call home confirmed his suspicion. Before Brian could tell his parents about his conversation with the coach, Coach Horton called home and spoke to his father, Jimmy. Jimmy Forrest finally slipped up. When Coach Horton called, he spoke of Brian's change in behavior. Mr. Forrest told Coach Horton that Brian's grandmother, who he was very close to, was dying of lung cancer and she had been pretty bad for a few weeks and just recently died.

Coach didn't call out the disparity in their conversations and Brian didn't tell his father of his error in their conversation that evening. Jimmy was extremely angry at Brian for allowing his emotions to show at school. He pulled him to the side and told him, "You better be glad that I covered for you. If you draw any more attention to yourself, you know your mother will pay. If he asks you any more questions, you tell him that you'll be okay and that your grandmother's death was hard on you."

"But, Jimmy," Brian started. Brian never referred to his father as "Father" or "Dad." He intended to tell Jimmy that he gave Coach Horton the excuse of fighting at home, but he wasn't given the opportunity.

"Brian, there are no buts. You better take your ass to school, do the best you can, and act normal. If I get any more phone calls home, this will be child's play compared to what comes next."

Uncle Cody, as usual, was nearby. "Jimmy, show him

how she will pay." Cody's request wasn't a demand or an order. It was more of a beg with excitement.

"Great idea, Code-man," Jimmy replied.

Jimmy called out to Sydney. As she arrived at the bedroom door, the look on everyone's face told her all she needed to know. Something was up and it wasn't good. She paused at the doorway and her face turned flush.

Jimmy pulled Brian's mother in the room by her hair and took the cigar from his mouth. Jimmy always had a cigar in his mouth. Brian detested that smell. That smell permeated the house and all of the vehicles, and it grew stronger as Jimmy came closer, and it was on Jimmy when Brian was violated by the disgusting excuse for a father. Jimmy took the lit cigar and pushed it into Sydney's forearm. She didn't make a sound, as she didn't want Brian to know that his actions had caused her pain, but Brian could see the pain in her eyes, which eventually started to weep.

Brian was quiet and, when his father left, ran to his mother and held her. Sydney said to him that she was sorry for everything and that she didn't want this for him. She begged him to stay strong so that she wouldn't be hurt anymore. Brian realized this manner of thinking was wrong. Shouldn't his mother be willing to do anything for him? Shouldn't a mother be willing to die to save her son? Although he loved his mother and realized she didn't want any of this for him, she did nothing to stop it. She put herself and her well-being ahead of him and his.

From his observations of animals, he knew his mother's way of thinking and lack of protection didn't even measure up to that of chickens. He had once had a pet hen that he witnessed being killed when she stepped between an attacking hawk and her chicks. She fought that hawk until the babies could escape, and by the time Brian had reached the fighting birds with a broom, the hawk had inflicted too much damage. "Henrietta" died as a result of those wounds.

Brian went back to school the next day and, for a few weeks, Coach Horton didn't say a word about anything. No one questioned the differences between his story and Jimmy's.

Each day in class, all was normal and Coach Horton didn't treat him any differently. School ended about three weeks after the phone call home and the burning incident. Coach Horton wished all of his students a wonderful summer and his best for their future. To the surprise of most, he announced his retirement at the end of the school year.

Coach Horton was a retiree from the United States Navy. He was a pilot in the Navy before he started his second career as a teacher. Piloting was his lifelong dream. When he first started flight school, he struggled greatly. He was nearly ready to quit until his father gave him some solid advice "Don't quit on your dream; make them take it from you." He continued with greater resolve and finally finished and fulfilled his lifelong desire of becoming an aviator.

He was a married man with two adult children of his own. One was a pilot in the Air Force. That piece of fruit didn't fall too far from the tree. His other son was a lawyer but, in his mind, that was a launching pad to the State Senate, U.S. Senate and, ultimately, the White House, much like his idol, Barack Obama.

Coach Horton was a teacher loved by all of his students and any of those that come in contact with him. He was a fairly large man at nearly six feet tall and two hundred pounds or so. According to national standards, he was overweight, but he was in fairly good shape despite the extra pounds. He even ran sprints with the high school football team during practice and all of the linemen had difficulty keeping up with him. That pained him a bit because, when he first started coaching, he was able to hang with the running backs and receivers and his current speed or rather lack of speed told him that no matter how fast he tried to run, age was catching up to him and he was getting older.

At the age of fifty-four, Coach Horton told people that he decided to call it quits after ten years of teaching to focus on his writing. Coach Horton had written three or four books but, in his mind, never really finished them and none of them were published. He wanted to get at least one completed before he got too old.

Twenty-two days after school let out and Coach

Horton had retired, there was a knock at the Forrest residence's front door. It was later than most would arrive at the door. The summer sun had set about an hour earlier. Jimmy Forrest was angered by the late unannounced disturbance and went to the door, snatching it open with fury in his eyes. He was met with a baseball bat across the face. The sound was like two pieces of wood banging together but slightly muffled. Jimmy stumbled back and eventually fell to the ground. Blood poured from his nose and mouth and he was lacking his full faculties.

Coach Horton, dressed head to toe in all black, quickly jumped on him and zip-tied his hands together, then stuffed a rag in his mouth and duct-taped it in place. Methodically, he moved up the stairs to the bedrooms. And, as if he had a sixth sense, walked straight into "Uncle Cody's" room, where he found him sound asleep. He took out his knife and grabbed him by the leg. Before Cody could react, Coach severed his right Achilles tendon. He wouldn't be running away from anyone or anything anytime soon. Just as the pain began to register in his sick and perverted brain, his skull met the same fate as Jimmy's. When sufficiently disabled, his hands were tied as well. A sock was stuffed in his mouth and duct tape was applied across his mouth and around his head.

Just then, Sydney emerged from her bedroom. She didn't scream or make a sound and, before she realized what was happening, her throat was cut. She dropped dead with very little pain and no reaction. As she slumped motionless to the floor, there was approval in her eyes and tears started to form in Coach Horton's eyes. This kill was the hardest. He knew this perverse mess wasn't her making, but she allowed it to happen in order to protect herself. Protecting Brian should have been her first priority, but it wasn't. She knew it, Brian knew it, and Coach Horton knew it as well.

Coach Horton made his way to Brian's room. There would be no pain here; no baseball bat and no knife. With Brian, Coach Horton took out a plastic bag. He opened the bag and pulled out a rag covered in ether. He placed it over Brian's mouth for a few seconds. He gently tied him up and carried him to the back door of the house.

It was time for the men to pay. He dragged Cody down the stairs by his hair. He had a head full of greasy blond hair that was longer than that of most women. Cody let out a yelp as his right foot hit each step. Coach thought he sounded like a whining Chihuahua. For some reason, this made Coach Horton chuckle a bit on the inside. He dragged him down the steps to the first floor and on to the basement and heard a muffled "yip, yip, yip" with each step, step, step. Once there, Coach H, as many referred to him, pulled a rope out and threw it over a rafter. He tied one end to Cody's hands and pulled him up until his arms were nearly pulled out of his shoulder sockets from behind his back. He anchored the rope and went to grab Jimmy. This would be a little more difficult. Moving over three hundred pounds of dead weight, though Jimmy wasn't dead, yet, wasn't easy for anyone. Even the most in-shape thirty-year-old man would find the task difficult, let alone a fifty-four-year-old man. He wrapped a rope around Jimmy's feet as he started to come to.

Coach H dragged Jimmy to the basement door. It was hard, but not impossible. Once he got to the door, Jimmy seemed to be hung up. When he looked, Jimmy was turned on his right side and had grabbed the door jamb with his left hand. Coach H, reached behind his back and out came the baseball bat again. One quick and precise swing broke Jimmy's left forearm. His grip was released and pulling him down the steps was easy. Each bump of that forearm on a step brought a sound similar to what Cody's leg did. "Yip, yip, yip." Coach H couldn't help but outright laugh this time.

There was no chance this pig would be hoisted. A pig... what a perfect word to describe Jimmy. He was fat like the literal pig and his sexual sickness made him a figurative pig. His suffering would take place on the floor. He grabbed the right ankle, tied a rope around it, threw the other end over a separate rafter from Cody's, and pulled as much as he could. He anchored that leg and took out another rope. The new rope was tied around Jimmy's left ankle. The other end was looped around a metal vertical support beam and pulled as far as it could. This put Jimmy in an awkwardly shaped split. A third rope was used to tie his hands to another vertical pole. This pig was ready to be filleted.

"Your actions have brought the wrath of God upon you. Cody, from what I have observed, you like to watch first, then take your turn. So you get to watch. You get to watch what's going to happen to you when your turn comes," Coach Horton stated as calmly and monotone as possible. "Jimmy, you sick fucking pig. You like to get it all started. So let's get started."

He pulled out an odd knife. Those who don't hunt probably wouldn't recognize the oddly shaped tool. It looked like a knife but not long and skinny. This one was nearly half as wide as it was long. Another odd part of this knife was the reversed sharpened hook on the spine of the knife. This part was designed to skin a deer or other animal while pulling the knife toward the knife's handler. The location of the hook allowed one to skin an animal without cutting into the flesh below.

Coach H used the hook to remove the outer garments from Jimmy. Jimmy seemed to know what was coming next as he tried to scream. The rag in his mouth let "Don't you fucking do it" come out as "Umm um ummumm um um." At this point, Coach H, made a slight cut in the skin on Jimmy's kneecap with the blade of the knife. Then, he dug the hook in and skinned Jimmy up to his groin. "UMMMMMMMMMM!!!" was all that Jimmy could utter before he passed out.

"Oh, it isn't going to be that easy for you," stated Coach H. He reached into his backpack, pulled out his tomahawk, and used it to crush Jimmy's left knee. Jimmy screamed in pain as he awoke. Coach took a few moments to let that pain sink in, then he destroyed the right kneecap. Next, he dug the hook a little deeper and pulled a little farther and ripped straight through Jimmy's scrotal sack. "You loved using this in such a wrong way. Let's just make this look as wrong as you used it." With that, he took the knife and came down with a chop to his manhood. He didn't slice it off; it was split in half lengthwise and blood poured out. Coach H then made a quick slice of Jimmy's femoral artery. Jimmy would be dead inside of ten minutes. As he looked over his shoulder, Coach H could see Cody squirming.

"Uncle Cody," he said. "You don't like what you see?"

Time was running long for Coach H. This one would have to be quicker. He took the knife and simply chopped between Cody's legs. He assumed he hit the mark, but he wasn't going to inspect his work. He then took the knife and stabbed Cody on the left side of his abdomen. He pulled the knife across to the right side, at which point, Cody's intestines fell to the floor. Cody passed out as he saw this. Coach H awoke him with the same blow to the left kneecap that was used to awaken Jimmy. He wanted Cody to experience more pain, albeit a short amount.

Once Cody was awake, Coach H paused a few moments then repeated the process with the right knee. Once Cody was writhing in pain, he pulled a half gallon jug from his backpack. He splashed the gasoline all around the two men. Next, he searched for anything flammable that he could in the basement. There was turpentine and some lighter fluid. He spread some of the turpentine around the basement. He used the lighter fluid to make a trail from the men up the stairs to the first floor and on up to Sydney's body on the second floor. He doused her in what was left of the gasoline and set her aflame. The lighter fluid allowed the flame to seemingly flow from Sydney, down the stairs, to the first floor and down the basement steps to the pig and his sick friend. They erupted into flames.

He went to the back door and grabbed Brian. He carried him over the chain link fence in the backyard that led to a vacant house. He moved quickly to his car parked in the driveway under a carport. He popped the trunk, which was purposely missing a light, and gently placed Brian inside. He jumped into the front seat and started the car. Leaving the lights off, he drove away. Once he got down the block, he turned his lights on and headed to his cabin in the mountains. Of course, Brian witnessed none of this. He was made aware of it all sometime later when Coach Horton told him.

Waiting there for them at the cabin was Mrs. Horton. Brian thought he had been dragged out of the frying pan and into the fire, but Mrs. Horton had a look about her and a way with words that allowed him to be comforted.

A man has a hard time keeping secrets from his wife. Mrs. Horton was well aware of Coach Horton's past. In fact, when their children were born, Coach Horton made her promise that she would put a bullet through his head if she ever caught him doing anything bordering on sexual abuse to their children. She promised. She was also very aware of his responsibility and she was there to help to raise Brian. The Horton children would know Brian for what he essentially was, a foster child and their brother. Mrs. Horton was there to comfort Brian when he was struggling with his past. Once when Brian was having an especially hard day, Mrs. Horton pulled Brian aside with Coach looking on and said, "Use the hurt, the anger, the sadness. Use it all to fuel you to be a better man. Use it to become a weapon in body and mind. Use it to fuel your workouts. Use it to fuel your studies. Use it to make you love those that love you with that much more love."

Brian looked over at Coach and directed his question directly to him "Is that what you did?"

Coach Horton told him this: "Brian, everything that has happened to you once happened to me. I used to blame God for what happened to me until my adopted father Chester told me. 'There are two people you can't blame for these things. You and God. You did as you were supposed to do. You loved and trusted your parents. God sent me to rescue you from them when they didn't do what God had entrusted them to do.' He also gave me that little tidbit of advice that Mrs. Horton just gave you. Since then, I stopped blaming God and myself and used everything as fuel to become who I am."

"So your parents abused you too?"

"Yes, they did."

Coach Horton began to tell him his story.

Chapter 7
Coach is Rescued

Coach Horton was born Alvin Horton in Little Rock, Arkansas. His parents were kind and loving. His father, Willie, was one of the few African Americans that worked in the industrial district. Willie was married to the lovely Maxine, who ran a dry-cleaners. They had six children between them, and Alvin Horton, the baby of the bunch, knew nothing but love: the love of his parents and the love of his three big brothers and two sisters. He was a bright student that loved to read. His family encouraged his reading activities. His parents and older siblings always bought him books. Among his favorites were the *Chronicles of Narnia* and *The Screwtape Letters* by C.S. Lewis and anything of the science-fiction variety, whether it be *I, Robot* by Isaac Asimov, *I Am Legend* by Richard Matheson, or any of a number of short stories.

One day in July of 1957, Alvin's life was flipped upside down. The summer heat along with the forced integration of schools had gotten to the residents of Little Rock. As the "Little Rock Nine" were escorted to school, two crowds formed. One crowd, which consisted mostly of African Americans, were there to show support for the teenagers. The other crowd, exclusively Caucasian, was there in protest. Alvin's father was there in support of the teenagers, and when one of his coworkers from the other side saw him, he threw a glass bottle at him. The bottle struck Alvin's father in the temple. Although the injury appeared minimal at the time, he suffered a massive stroke not long after the event. He clung to life for two weeks, but, despite being a strong man and fighting with all his might, he lost the battle. He was laid to rest on Alvin's eleventh birthday.

His mother lost the laundromat after paying for his father's hospital bill. Without income to support the family,

Alvin and two of his siblings ended up in foster care. Most found homes right away, including Alvin. The Andersen couple that took Alvin in were known as a good, religious family. He was adopted by them about six months after his father's death. His mother agreed to the adoption because she knew Alvin would have a better life with his new "well-to-do" family. Not long after he was adopted, the family moved to a farm in the hills of Kentucky. That was when everything changed.

Not one week after the move, Alvin was awakened by someone crawling into his bed. At first, he thought it was the family's German shepherd. He was shocked to realize it was his new father.

"P-Paul, what are you doing?"

"Francine kicked me out of bed. Can I sleep here?"

"Ohhhh-kay," he replied with uncertainty.

The next night, it was the same. This time, his father cuddled with him. Each night, this continued until Alvin's new father touched him inappropriately.

"What are you doing?"

"Don't you love me?" his father asked.

"I-I do, but…"

"I love you too. When people love one another, it's okay for them to touch each other. Like Francine and I do."

"That's not how I was raised. This is wrong."

"Doesn't the Bible say honor thy mother and father?"

"It does."

"This is honoring me."

Alvin never felt comfortable with this man's actions. Later, his new "mother" joined in on the activities. He felt dirty. When it came time to go to school, his parents didn't send him. When they moved to Kentucky, there was no evidence that he existed. There was no legal need to educate him or send him to school. He was, in just about every sense of the word, a prisoner in his new home. More appropriately put, he was a sex slave to his adopted parents. He hated his life. He knew it was wrong, but he was powerless over his parents. He lived miserably in the house, secluded from everything on the outside. There was no internet or cable television in those days. The only connection to the outside world he had were the three network stations and two local stations. There was a house phone, but his parents kept the handset locked up and it was for their use only.

The farm sat on the plateau of a small mountain. The "flat top" of the mountain was approximately three and a half acres in area. Beyond the plateau, there were sheer cliffs with 150-foot drop-offs. The family got up and down to the house in a ski lift. After about a two-hundred-yard ride in the lift, a passenger would arrive at a parking lot, which connected to roads up and down the mountain. Further along the lift, one could actually ski in the winter time.

The house had been built and owned by a moonshiner who once ran the industry in that part of the country. He lived in constant fear of revenge from those he had hurt, his competitors and more realistically, the law. He figured that living in such a manner would make any attack on him and his family extremely difficult. It turned out that the ski lift, though it offered protection for his property, had no protection itself and one of those individuals with which he was concerned put a bullet through his head as he was riding the lift down to his vehicle. No one knew who actually pulled the trigger. Alvin's new father was a distant nephew of the moonshiner and inherited the property. There was no mortgage owed on the property and all he needed to do in order to keep the house was to pay yearly taxes on it.

The abuse continued and Alvin found a way to endure the pain. He left. He couldn't leave in the physical sense. That was impossible, but he would leave in his mind. He would go somewhere he had once read about in one of his books. Each time, he would go to a different place. One day, it was Narnia; another time, it would be aboard the *Nautilus*. Once in that place, his body wasn't his and what happened to it didn't happen to him.

He wasn't sure of the exact time periods of any of this as he didn't have a calendar or go to school or watch television to keep track of the days. One day, a man came that Alvin had never seen before. Alvin wasn't sure what to make of the man. He thought, perhaps, that he was going to be "given" to him as his "parents" were very friendly with the man and kept talking about all of Alvin's physical attributes. Alvin got himself ready for what was to come. He prepared for his journey, this time, to the deep sea aboard Captain Nemo's submarine, the *Nautilus*. But something was different with this man. He walked up to Alvin and asked him a simple question. "Are you okay?"

"Sir?"

"Are you okay?"

Alvin didn't know how to answer.

"Son, are you okay?"

"No, I'm not," Alvin volunteered.

"I didn't think so," the stranger replied. With that, the stranger reached inside his jacket and pulled out his tomahawk. Before Alvin's "parents" knew what was happening, they were hit in the head with the weapon. The father was struck first, the mother was next. The impact disabled each of them. They were still conscious but were incapacitated, dazed, and confused.

The stranger quickly used leather straps from the other inside jacket pocket to tie up Alvin's adoptive parents. Once they were tied, the stranger took Alvin outside.

"Young man, I am here to free you from this way of life. I promise you that I will never do the things to you that these people have done. I am offering you a chance at a life without abuse. It is your choice to accept this life or not. I am going to send you down the lift. Then I am going to go inside and make sure these people never hurt anyone ever again. If you want to come with me, send the lift back up and stay in my car. If not, go wherever you want to go. I will find my way back to my car and I will move on with my life without you. This is your choice."

The stranger put him on the ski lift and sent him on his way. As the ski lift carried the newly liberated Alvin, he turned in the chair and asked one question. "What's your name?"

"If you send the lift back and are in my car when I

return, I will tell you my name and everything about me."

The trip to the car lasted about four minutes. It didn't take a fourth of that time for Alvin to make his decision. He didn't know this man. He didn't know his intentions, but he knew what he had gone through the last year or so and he knew that whatever this man had in store for him couldn't be any worse. He would go with the man. Once he was at the level with the cars, he flipped the switch to send the chair back up the hill, walked to the man's car, climbed in, and waited.

Meanwhile, the stranger re-entered the house, walked up to the woman, and said to her, "You are a sorry excuse for a woman and mother." With that statement, he used the tomahawk to nail four spikes into the floor and took the woman and spread her out on the floor and tied her hands and feet to the spikes. He moved to the man. Before he did anything, he struck the man in his left kneecap with the weapon. The kneecap shattered and the man screamed in agony as he left his state of conscious dazedness. He lifted the man and placed him in a chair and tied him down. For good measure, he used the tomahawk on the right kneecap. Again, the man screamed in agony as his kneecap was shattered.

The stranger moved to the woman. "Anything you want, you can have it. Take the boy; he is yours," she pleaded.

He lifted his pants leg and removed his knife from its sheath tied to his left calf. He moved to her and cut her abdomen. The cut was deep enough to cut the skin and some of the muscle below it but not deep enough to get to her intestines below. She called out her husband's name in agony, at which point, the husband said to the stranger, "Do you know who you're messing with? You will be dead before you leave this mountain."

"Do I look like I am afraid? Do you know who I am?" the stranger replied in a monotone, non-emotional voice. "Your actions have brought the wrath of God upon you."

He went to the man and made a similar-depth cut on his legs from his knees to his groin. The man screamed and wiggled as the cut was made. The stranger thought of the boy. What was going through his mind? Was he waiting in the car or did he go somewhere to try to find a different option? If he was waiting while the stranger did his damage, how long would he wait? The stranger sped up his process. He went back to the woman and made two deep slashes to her face. Again, she screamed and, again, the man threatened him.

The stranger went back to the man and continued his previous cut. He extended the cut through the man's scrotum and filleted his manhood. The man screamed and passed out. A little tap on the left knee caused enough pain to bring him back around. Next, the man raised his right pants leg and pulled out a flask filled with gasoline. He splashed the gasoline on the two molesters and then he went to the bedroom and grabbed some of the woman's hairspray. He returned to his victims, took a lighter out of his pocket, and lit it. He held the flame in front of him about a foot from the woman's gas-soaked face. In his other hand, he held the hairspray. He pushed the can's actuator and the spray was released. As it hit the flame, it ignited much like a flame thrower. The flame continued to the woman's face, which ignited the gasoline. In short order, her upper torso was a aflame like a bonfire of a molesting woman. He moved to the man and ignited him in the same fashion. He took off his jacket and used it to smother the flames on the woman. Once her flame was extinguished, he used the jacket on the man. Both were severely burned but still alive. The man left them there to suffer in agony and walked outside. He was pleasantly surprised to see the lift in place. He rode the lift down to his car, opened the driver's side door, and climbed into the seat. He started the car and said, "Chester Tiberius Jackson."

"Huh?" replied Alvin.

"You asked for my name. My name is Chester Tiberius Jackson."

Chester took Alvin to his cabin in the mountains of Virginia. When they arrived, Alvin was uncertain. He thought to himself, *Out of the frying pan and into the fire.* Chester could see the concern in Alvin's eyes.

Chester looked at Alvin. "Young man," he said, "Look at me. Look into my eyes so you can see that what I am telling you is the truth."

Alvin looked at Chester, then he looked away.

"Son, look at me."

This time, Alvin focused on Chester's eyes. "Alvin, everything that has happened to you once happened to me. I used to blame God for what happened to me. One day, you may do the same. My adopted father told me. 'There are two people you can't blame for these things. You and God. You did as you were supposed to do. You loved and trusted your adopted parents. God sent me to rescue you from them when they didn't do what God had entrusted them to do."

Alvin could see in Chester's eyes that he was telling the truth.

"How did you find me?"

"Kid, I'm resourceful and observant. Until a month ago, I worked at the general store in town. I noticed Paul and Francine coming into the store over a period of time buying kids' clothes and shoes but never saw a kid. One day, I followed them to the mountain but drove past as they made their turn. The next night, I climbed the backside of the mountain and looked around. When I took a look inside, I saw you sitting on the bed, crying, and Paul leaving the room and pulling up his pants. At that point, I knew what was going on. From that moment until yesterday, I was planning and getting ready for your rescue. I quit my job."

Chester's voice changed for the next sentence to show that what was to follow wasn't the truth. "To go help my sick mother in Ohio." His voice returned to normal. "That's when I bought the place we're heading to. It's secluded for our privacy."

Alvin looked unsure.

Chester's voice changed again. This time, it was assuring. "Son, I… am … not ... going … to … hurt … you. We are going to go heal. I told you, I've been in your shoes. I know what you've gone through. I bet you 'left' (Chester held up air quotes) when it was happening."

Alvin was taken aback. *How does he know that?* he thought.

Chester could see Alvin's surprise. "Son, I've been there."

Finally, Alvin relented. Everything came out. The death of his father, the look on his mother's face when it became more than apparent that she could no longer care for him, the first time Paul touched him; all if it came out in a guttural scream followed by tears. These were not ordinary tears; this was a snot-filled sob.

Chester wanted to hug the young man but knew from experience that was the last thing Alvin could take. He simply reached into his pocket and pulled out a handkerchief and gave it to Alvin.

Alvin was raised as Chester's orphaned nephew. After a year of healing and tutelage under Chester's care, he was able to get back on track with his education and he finished high school on time. In his twenties, he grew fascinated with the novels and television series based on the adventures of Captain James T. Kirk and the crew of NCC-1701, the USS *ENTERPRISE*. *Star Trek* wasn't an obsession, but it became a dream of his to venture into space. He wasn't able to "go where no man has gone before," but he was able to become a Naval Aviator and that was close enough.

Chapter 8
Paying the Debt

When Brian made it back to the RV, his mind was clear and he was back on task. He knew what had to be done and why. His focus was strengthened and he would not be distracted anymore.

Brian took a shower and prepared his kit. In a backpack, he put all the tools he knew he'd need: zip-ties for hands and feet, duct tape, two rags, an additional ether-soaked rag in a ziplock bag, rope to hoist, a skinning knife, a half-gallon container of gasoline, a drill, and half a dozen screw-in eye bolts, ammonia capsules, a small fire extinguisher, and finally, a stun baton that was a modern substitute for a baseball bat. The stun baton was a foot and a half long metal pipe that could be used to hit someone over the head and on the end of it was a stun gun that could disable someone with an electrical shock. This was two weapons in one and fit nicely into the backpack.

Once all was prepared, he put his motorcycle back on its rack on the back of the RV and took a nap. This was going to be a long night, not only for the Creasys but for himself as well.

After a nap, Brian settled up with the RV park and told them that he planned on leaving that evening.

At 10 p.m., he pulled out of the RV park and headed for a Waffle House that wasn't more than five miles from the Creasy house. He had made a stop here on his dry run and once on his way back after the scouting trip. He took his time to eat and conducted some idle chitchat with the waitress and cook. In all, he spent the better part of an hour and a half there. That wasn't enough. He needed to burn more time. He couldn't take the RV to the Creasy driveway until after midnight. His plan was to drive to the Creasy property and turn off his lights as he started down the driveway. He would drive seventy-five yards down the driveway. This would put the RV far enough from the road as to not draw attention and far enough from the house as to not alert the Creasys.

How to burn more time? The answer was simple. He headed to a nearby LowMart. He was careful to park with the rear license plates out of view of any cameras. Once inside, he walked around for a bit, and eventually, made his way to the grocery section, where he bought some food, chips, drinks, toilet paper, etc. After burning an hour in LowMart, he headed for the checkout. He paid for the items with cash. This entire trip was paid for with cash except for the tourist attractions. He didn't want his credit card to document his presence near the Creasy residence.

While in the parking lot, he made a quick check of the Creasy cameras and microphones. All was quiet on the Creasy front. It was time to move. He put on his clothes. He dressed himself from head to toe in black. Had someone seen him, they might have thought he was ready for a Halloween Party dressed as a ninja without the headgear.

He headed down the road toward the Creasy residence. Again, he made sure there was no traffic in front of him or behind. He got to the Creasy driveway undetected and everything was going as planned. He went to his blind, collected his gear, and took it to the RV.

It was time to head to the property. Once there, he placed the trusty .45 caliber model 1911 in his holster that neatly fit under his right arm, ready to be used by his left hand if needed. He departed the RV and collected all the cameras and microphones and the transmitter from the nearby tree. The cleanup was done. It was time to go to work. He rerouted the phone lines, so any call to an alarm company went nowhere, but the alarm company could pulse the system and no interruptions would be detected. This was a safety move. He didn't plan on setting off any alarms, but he couldn't risk a slip-up. Then he cut the perimeter of the basement window. There would be no broken glass sound and the magnetic trigger wouldn't move. Climbing through this hole in the window wouldn't normally be an easy task, but given the size of this window, it wasn't too difficult for a man as limber as Brian.

He was in. Now it was time to pay the debt. As he approached the stairs, he saw a weed whacker leaning on a nearby wall. He had an idea. He picked it up.

As he passed the parents' room, he dropped off the weed whacker just outside their room. It wasn't time for them just yet. His first stop was Tyler's room. He didn't want the boy to be awoken to the horror that was to come. He figured if his trip to Tyler caused the boy's mother or father to wake up, he could disable them in no time and injuring them would not do the same kind of emotional damage to Tyler that waking up to the parents' next agonizing twenty minutes would.

Once in the room, he took out the ether-soaked rag and placed it over Tyler's nose and mouth. After a few seconds, he was able to see the change in Tyler that let Brian know that he was no longer sleeping. Rather, he was "knocked out."

Next, it was time for the adults. He went straight to Eric Creasy, took out his stun baton, placed it on his neck, and pushed the button. Eric let out a quick yelp as he went into convulsions and was knocked out. The sound woke Tammy. Just as she came to, Brian gave her a shock as well. She was out just as quick as Eric.

Brian pulled the zip-ties from his backpack and tied Eric's hands behind his back. Then it was on to Tammy. He zip-tied her hands in the same fashion then tied her legs. He went back to Eric and zip-tied his legs, stuffed a rag in his mouth, and wrapped duct tape around his head and over his mouth. He repeated the process with Tammy. This would definitely silence the pair, which was a bit of overkill, since the location of this house wouldn't let screams bring any unwanted attention. But the main purpose of the rag was to make both Eric and Tammy feel as helpless as Tyler and their other victims felt.

Next, he took out his drill and carefully found the studs above and drilled two holes into the ceiling. He inserted the eyebolts in the holes and screwed them in. As he was finishing the second bolt, Eric started to come to. Another quick jolt from the stun gun put him out again. He tied a rope around each of Tammy's hands and cut the zip-tie. He ran the first rope through an eyebolt and pulled it tight. He did the same with the second hand. When he was done, she was hanging from the ceiling by her hands. He then drilled holes in the floor and repeated the process with her legs. She awoke about thirty seconds after she was made into a human X hanging from the ceiling and tied to the floor. When she woke up, she tried to scream, but all that came out were muffled noises silenced by the rag.

He moved to Eric. With Eric, he grabbed a nearby wooden chair and placed him in it and made him face "Tammy X." He duct-taped his hands to the arms of the chair and his ankles to the legs of the chair. He also used a rope to tightly tie his torso to the chair. He noticed a small double-barreled shotgun in the corner of the room. Obviously, it was there for home protection. This made him laugh a bit. Upon inspection, he found that it was a loaded .410 shotgun. The shells in the gun were birdshot. This was powerful enough to slow a man down, but unless he was hit in the head, it probably wouldn't kill him.

A bit of deviance snuck up on Brian. He took the shotgun and placed it on the floor and pointed it at Eric's groin. He secured it in place with duct tape and set it up with some paracord he had in his backpack. It was rigged in such a way that, if Eric moved his left arm more than an inch, the gun would go off. He then loosened the duct tape on Eric's left hand a bit.

It was time to get them ready for cleaning up any evidence he might leave behind. He pulled out the gasoline from his backpack and poured some over Tammy's head so that it dripped down to cover her body and then he poured it all over Eric.

"Oh no, it isn't going to be that easy." Brian took the tomahawk from his backpack and swung it with full force against Tammy's knee. She awoke and screamed in pain. As she sobbed, he walked over to Eric and brought the tomahawk down on his left knee. The great pain caused Eric to wake up in a groggy panic.

There he tortured them and moved on rescue Tyler.

* * *

He grabbed Tyler and carried him down the stairs towards the front door. He disarmed the alarm with the code he had observed the family punch in a few times over the last two days and walked out the front door. He stopped dead in his tracks. "I can't believe I almost forgot it." He gently laid Tyler down on the grass and ran to the boy's bedroom. Once there, he disconnected the Xbox and threw it into his backpack. He ran back down the stairs and out the door. He picked up Tyler and made his way to the RV.

Once there, he put Tyler in the bed in the back and tied him down. He hated to do this and the part that would come next even more. He placed a rag in his mouth and secured it with duct tape. This boy was going to wake up in a crazy state and this was no way to develop trust; but he couldn't have him wake up and start screaming and draw attention to the odd pair. He had to make it to the cabin before he could set Tyler free and that was a good twelve-hour drive. With any luck, he'd be out most of the trip.

No such luck. Three hours into the trip, Brian could hear Tyler struggling in the back of the RV. He was violent in his attempt to get free. Brian was afraid Tyler would hurt himself. He pulled off of the highway at the next exit and drove down the road for a little bit until he found a secluded spot and parked the RV. He went to the back and saw Tyler nearly out of the ropes and having almost forced the rag out of his mouth over the duct tape. *This kid is a fighter*, he thought.

"Tyler, calm down. I am not here to hurt you. I am here to help. I know what was going on at your house. I need you to relax."

Tyler didn't begin to slow down.

"Look, dude, I'm SurfGod, your SurfBro."

Tyler froze with a puzzled look on his face.

"Hold on a second." Brian went to retrieve his voice-altering box. "Hey, bro, let's kill some newbs," Brian said through the box, but the voice came out as the voice of the kid Tyler knew as SurfBro.

Tyler relaxed but looked confused.

"If you promise not to yell, I'll take that rag out. I know it is a little hard to breathe with it in."

Tyler nodded.

He took the rag out and Tyler asked, "My parents?"

Brian replied, "They won't hurt you anymore."

The tone said it all and Tyler understood.

"Tyler, my name is Brian. This is a long story and we'll have some time to get more acquainted, but we need to get on the road. Can I trust you to sit back here and watch some TV until we get to my house?"

"Rocky, we have to get Rocky."

"What?"

"Brian, I believe you are who you say you are. Even if you're not, what worse could you do to me? If I'm gone, they'll hurt or kill Rocky."

"Tyler, the deal is that I save one. At some point in my life, it was expected of me to save one. That one was you. My debt is paid."

"I don't know about your deal or your debt. Rocky is going to be hurt or killed. I'll go wherever you want to go and do whatever you want to do as long as we get Rocky. If not, I'll be loud, I'll scream, I'll fight… I might even kill myself."

"Calm down, kid. Who is Rocky? Do you even know where Rocky lives?"

"Rocky is a girl they made me… They made me do things with. They hurt her too." Tyler was beginning to cry. "She told me that they threatened to kill her if anyone ever found out about the things they did to her. My parents told me the same thing. She lives somewhere near Tupelo. Can I ask you something?"

"Sure."

"How did you find me?"

"Tyler, that is kind of a long story, but the short version is, I used Xbox and the internet to track your address."

"You did!?" Tyler asked excitedly.

"Yeah, I'm a computer guy, and at my job, doing stuff like tracking people over the internet is what I do."

"Then you can find Rocky."

"Come again?"

"She's one of my Xbox friends. You can use my Xbox to track her down."

Brian's mind began to race. Surely the FBI would be informed of the kidnapping; they'd begin to investigate; and they would find out about Rocky. It was only a matter of time, but how much time?

"Brian, we have to go get my Xbox."

"No, we don't," Brian replied.

"It's the only way to find her."

"I understand, but we don't have to go get your Xbox; it's right here." Brian reached down to the cabinet near his feet and pulled out the Xbox.

"Can you do it? Can you find Rocky?"

"It is going to be tricky. We need to make a stop or two first."

Brian knew this was the end of the road. Saving this girl would be the end of life as he knew it. He'd have to watch his back forever. There would be no FBI job; rather, he'd be hiding from the FBI and that was no easy task. His tracking of Rocky would have to be untraceable. He needed a way to find her without being found right away. He needed a burner phone with internet access. To purchase that phone, he couldn't use a credit card. The first stop was a drugstore to get a gift card. With the gift card, he could buy the "pay as you go" or "burner" phone with internet access. He would hook that phone up to the Xbox and track Rocky's IP address to her actual address.

He didn't have time to plan a clean escape for her. This would have to be a brutal smash and grab operation.

He pulled the RV into a drugstore parking lot. He didn't want to draw too much attention and he did what he could to avoid security cameras; hopefully, the hat and sunglasses would help enough.

"Tyler, you have to promise me. Promise me you won't get out of this RV. If you do, I am gone and you will never see me again. Rocky will most likely die, and you'll be picked up by the police and put in an orphanage, to end up who knows where, and I will be running from the police for the rest of my life. So, promise me."

"I promise. I just want Rocky safe. I'll do whatever you need to make that happen."

Brian did according to plan and all went well. He purchased the gift card with cash. He, then purchased the phone with 5GB of data. When he finished everything, he returned to the RV. At first, he didn't see Tyler, and for a moment, that fight or flight response kicked in. He had that sickening feeling in his stomach. Just when he thought he was going to have to make a run for it, Tyler opened the bathroom door and walked out.

"Man, am I glad to see you."

"I told you I wasn't going anywhere, but when nature calls, who am I to question the call."

Brian was amazed at Tyler's resilience, joking now after all of this and what was to come. This told Brian that this kid was either a psychopath or amazingly strong. He knew in his soul it was the latter.

Brian hooked up the Xbox and the phone. He let Tyler log in to his Xbox Live account. As soon as he was in, Brian ran the trace and got Rocky's address. This whole operation took less than five minutes. Brian knew this would raise no flags as no one would know that Tyler was missing just yet..

"Okay, Tyler, we have her address and I am going to do what I can to get her out. You have to do what I say, no more and no less."

"SurfBro, I got you. You are the boss."

Brian drove the RV to the parking lot of an abandoned grocery store near the Tupelo address. It was now five hours since Brian had rescued Tyler.

He was tired, uncertain, and his head was racing. The uncertainty of this rescue made him very uncomfortable. He had rehearsed and been trained on how to rescue Tyler for years.

Tyler's rescue appeared to be unrehearsed, but the

steps to make a rescue were driven into Brian's BEING by Coach Horton through years of practice and rehearsal and "The Way." "The Way" gave him the steps to follow: how to enter a house, what to pack, what to wear, what time of night to enter, how to make the offenders pay, and on and on.

Brian would be flying by the seat of his pants with this one. It went against everything he had been taught, but two things led him to make this rescue. One was Tyler. The other was Brian witnessing her abuse. Deep down inside, he wanted to make this rescue as well. Although Tyler's rescue put him into the black with his debt, he felt an obligation to rescue Rocky as well.

There was no time to rest, no time to gain intelligence on the family by staking it out. There was no time to wait until nightfall. He had to move before the FBI showed up here. He knew his job. He knew his people. He knew time was limited. Brian fell back on his training to make the preparations for this hurried rescue. He knew he had to travel light and quick. His backpack would be almost empty this time. It contained two things, his stun baton and a quart of gasoline. He did carry one other item and this is the part he hated. He carried a silenced .45 caliber 1911 semi-automatic pistol. This gun was an original 1911 used as a service pistol by his "great-grandfather" or the preceding three generations of rescuer. Fortunately, this gun did not have a "fingerprint" submitted by the manufacturer. But matched bullets have sealed the fate of countless murders when the guns were recovered. That meant that this gun could never be found in his possession should he use it in this case.

Brian pulled up the address on the burner phone's GPS application and took a look at the lay of the land. There was good news and bad. This was a similar property without any neighbors for a good distance. The bad news was the driveway was long and the inhabitants might be alerted to his arrival. His other concern was how to get Rocky to come with him.

"Tyler, is there anything I can tell Rocky to let her know I am on her side and that I know you? Something that only the two of you know?"

Tyler thought for a few seconds. "Yes, tell her that

Nube Slayer says no more fat dudes."

"What's that all about?"

"When we play Xbox, I always go after the newbies. She calls me Nube Slayer. And the fat dudes. Well, she hates everything that our parents put us through, but the fat dudes make it so she can't breathe and that scares her."

Brian told Tyler the same thing he told him before he left for the drug store. "You promise?"

"I promise."

"If I'm not back in forty-five minutes, you take the money that is under the bed, take the I.D. that's in there with the money. Wear a baseball hat wherever you go. Pull it down on your head as far as it can go. That will help hide your face. You find your way to a bus station and buy a ticket to Philadelphia. When you get there, you call the number on this piece of paper and tell whoever answers 'my chain is broken, Brian said you can fix it.' Got it?"

"Yes, I have it."

"What do you say to the person on the phone?"

"The chain is broken."

"No, MY chain is broken, Brian said you can fix it."

"MY chain is broken, Brian said you can fix it."

"Forty-five minutes. I'll see you."

Brian started on the motorcycle. He rode up to the address, careful to have no traffic too close. He made it to the driveway without traffic and drove straight down the driveway. There was no time to park the motorcycle and walk.

Inside the house, Billy Monroe and Steve Williams were discussing college football.

"Mississippi State is going to be a powerhouse this year, man," stated Billy. However, the "man" at the end of the sentence was pronounced more like "may-yen." Billy had a habit of ending just about every third sentence with that word and pronounced that way, may-yen. It drove most of those that knew him crazy. Because of his stature and reputation, no one ever said anything about his annoying speech pattern.

"What do you mean by 'powerhouse?'" Steve inquired.

"I mean they are going to challenge 'Bama for the title in the SEC West."

"Are you telling me that Mississippi State is going to beat Nick Saban's *Crimson Tide* this year?"

"I'm sayin' they are going to have a record just as good as Alabama this year, may-yen. And they may even win the West. It may come down to their head-to-head matchup and State might just win this year, may-yen!" Billy was getting excited, and the more excited he became, the more frequent the "may-yens" became.

The two men heard the sound of a vehicle heading down the gravel driveway.

"Billy, go see who that is and get them the hell out of here."

"Okay, may-yen."

Billy walked outside to see who was coming down the driveway. He was pissed. *How dare someone come to my home uninvited*, he thought.

When Brian got to the house, he was greeted by Billy. He didn't know the man's name, but he thought to himself, *This is one of the biggest men I have ever seen.* This wasn't the one that Brian assumed was the father from the Creasy house. This man was present at the Creasys' and took part in the abuse, though.

"Can I help you, may-yen?" Billy asked.

I know that may-yen. This is that sick son of a bitch from the house, Brian thought.

Brian said, "Yeah, I have a package for a James Weeden."

"There's no one here by that na..."

Before the "m" was pronounced in the word "name," a bullet from the "silenced," or suppressed, .45 caliber handgun ripped through this large man's skull. Billy was dead before his body fell to the ground.

Brian walked to the front door and opened it. From another room, he heard, "Billy, who the fuck was that?"

Brian didn't answer, but he went toward the male voice. As he turned the corner to the kitchen, the man started again, "Billy, who..." Before he could start the next word, he looked up just in time to see the trigger pulled. Before he could register what was happening and even react to make a run for it, a bullet penetrated his throat and severed his spinal cord as it exited the back of his neck. His head was nearly severed by this one shot, but he didn't die. However, he couldn't move and his heart stopped.

Brian could see there was still life in the eyes of Rocky's father and the look of surprise was still on his face. *No matter*, he thought. *He will be dead in a few seconds.* "Your actions have brought the wrath of God upon you," Brian said as he left him there to die.

Two down, how many to go?

Brian made a sweep of the bottom floor and found no one there. He started up the stairs. As he got to the top, a naked man emerged from a bedroom heading to what appeared to be the bathroom. He didn't make it that far. Out of the corner of his eye, he caught a glimpse of someone moving. His reaction was to turn his head toward Brian. When he locked his gaze on Brian, the .45 caliber round was on its way to him at a velocity of 1,225 ft/s, too fast for him to react or avoid it hitting him right between his eyes. He dropped without taking a step or making a sound.

When Brian got to the top of the stairs, he could see a young teenaged girl in the room from which the naked man had just emerged. She was wearing very little and had wrapped herself in a sheet. She looked terrified and like she was trying to scream but just couldn't.

Brian held one finger to his lips and made the "Shhh" sound. He whispered, "Are you Rocky?"

The girl nodded.

"My name is Brian. Nube Slayer says no more fat dudes."

This puzzled her for a moment. Then she gave a slight grin.

"Is there anyone else up here?" Brian was still whispering.

"I don't know. Billy and my dad are here somewhere, but no one else is here. My mom is at the store."

"I need you to get dressed. Quickly, put on some jeans, a t-shirt, a sweatshirt. Grab some tennis shoes or boots. Do you have a backpack?"

"Yes, in the closet."

Brian grabbed it. "Put some more clothes in here. Underwear, bras, and another pair of pants and a couple of shirts. We'll get some more clothes later. Rocky, I need you to hurry."

She quickly got dressed and packed her bag.

"Okay, I need you to trust me."

"Trust is hard for me, but I really want to get out of here and you can't do any worse to me than what they have done."

Almost Tyler's exact words, he thought.

"Fair enough. Please take this scarf and wrap it around your eyes. There is some stuff downstairs that I don't want you to see."

"If it is anything like Thomas on the floor right there, it isn't going to bother me. Brian, the things I have seen, done, and have had done to me make this nothing."

"Okay. Then do this… I want you to go straight out the front door and go sit on my motorcycle. I need to clean some things up. How long until your mom gets back?"

"I don't know. Twenty minutes or so."

"We need to hurry."

Rocky stepped over Thomas and spat on him as she passed over him and headed out the door. As she passed Billy, she spat on him too. Brian knew both of these men had harmed her. This must have been her little bit of getting back at them. Once she was on the motorcycle, Brian grabbed Billy's feet and dragged him inside the house. He went back upstairs and doused Thomas, as Rocky referred to him, with gasoline. He lit him on fire and headed to the kitchen. He did the same with Rocky's presumed father and on his way out the door. Finally, he doused Billy with gasoline and lit the human candle. He gave Rocky his spare helmet, put on his helmet, and headed down the driveway.

When he got to the end of the driveway, he turned onto the road and headed to the RV When he got there, thirty minutes from the moment he left, he was greeted by an excited Tyler.

"Brian, you did it. You got her. Rocky, we're free!"

"Guys, I need both of you in the RV. Get in, close the door, and stay out of sight. I need to put the motorcycle up and we need to get out of here."

Brian secured the motorcycle and they started down the road. Just as they turned onto the main road, Rocky spotted her mother and told Brian.

"My mother just went by."

"Okay. There's nothing we can do to or for her now. We have to get going."

"I want her... I want her to suffer the way I did."

"Rocky, she will. Someway, somehow, she will suffer. Her husband is dead and any investigation into this incident will reveal what they did to you. She will go to prison and she will be abused in there for the rest of her life. Prison has a way of settling things up for those that abuse children. Even criminals have standards. If I am wrong and she doesn't go to prison, I will come back one day and finish the job. I promise."

Brian drove through the night and into the next morning. He only stopped for gas. On the trip, he continually ate sunflower seeds and drank soda. This was a trick he had learned from Coach H. Coach H found that eating seeds and drinking soda kept him awake on those late night "bags," or flights, in the Navy. When they finally arrived at the cabin, he was exhausted. He told his two rescued victims to pick rooms and get some sleep. He would explain everything the next morning.

The children agreed. They were free; at least, they felt that way. They went into the selected rooms and each child slept more soundly than they had in years.

Chapter 9
The Feds Arrive

Once Chief Caldwell realized a child was missing, his first call was to the FBI regional office. They told him that a team was on the way. That didn't stop Chief Caldwell from conducting his own investigation. The FBI would be investigating the missing child and apparent kidnapping aspect of the case. He would be conducting an investigation into the murders. At least, that was his official role. Really, he was investigating the whole damn thing. That was what took him to the residence of Jackson Holmes.

When he saw the video and got the information from Jackson, he called the FBI agents to set up a meeting. They met in the station's conference room.

"Ladies and gents, this case has gotten more crazy than the murders and kidnapping, if you can believe that. We have found DVDs of some pretty sick stuff, children having sex with one another and groups of men and women taking turns with children. Our investigation has led us to find that Tyler communicated his abuse to only one known person, a kid named Jackson. According to Jackson, Tyler did have one friend that suffered with him, a girl with a nickname of 'Rocky.' Her real name is unknown. Jackson said that Tyler and Rocky communicated over Xbox. Our search for the Xbox has come up empty. So far, that's what we have. Oh, and the approximate one hundred grand of marijuana in the shed in the backyard."

"Chief, we appreciate your input and, in full disclosure, we haven't been as lucky," Agent Rigby replied. "We have searched the property and found tracks of a large vehicle, possibly a large truck or SUV. We have reviewed every tape of every traffic camera and security camera in the area. There is nothing that resembles anything out of the ordinary. Unfortunately, there aren't any cameras that are limited to the immediate area of the Creasy home. The only cameras are those up the road about a mile. Those cameras show all kinds of trucks and cars moving, but nothing out of the ordinary, no indication of children at that time of night. One of our problems is that once you get to the end of the road, there are fifteen different ways out of this town and only two contain cameras. We are canvassing the area to see if anyone has noticed anything out of the ordinary."

Reggie spoke up. "Excuse me, Chief, I'm just thinking out loud here. I play Xbox all the time. Agent Rigby, is there some way to find out who this kid was talking to on Xbox? If someone took it, there is a reason, right? Can we find out who his Xbox friends are and maybe even find this 'Rocky' girl?"

"Thank you, Reggie. Good thinking." Chief Caldwell was going to ask the same question, but he didn't want to step on Reggie's toes. "Well, gentlemen, is there a way to get this information?"

"We'll contact our Cyber Crimes Division and see what they can get for us."

The Cyber Crimes Division promised to get started on the Xbox research as soon as they could. Being a man down, they had some backlogged cases; however, they promised to get to it in no less than twenty-four hours.

A day later, Agent Rigby was contacted by Agent Ford of the Cyber Crimes Division. She was given the rundown.

"We started with an attempt to track the Creasys' credit cards to an Xbox Live account; however, none of their credit cards matched an account."

"Next, we traced the IP address from the Creasys' Xbox internet connection to connections the Xbox made. There were several that came up. One traced to a home just outside Tupelo, Mississippi about two hours away from the Creasys' house. A few more were scattered throughout the world from places as close as Little Rock, Arkansas to as far away as Bahrain. Only two had routine consistency. The one in Tupelo was connected three to four times a week from five minutes to an hour at a time. One more connected to an address in Jamestown, Virginia with the same frequency pattern as the one in Tupelo, but he never connected to both at the same time."

Jamestown, Virginia was a small town outside Norfolk and was known as the first English settlement in the United States. The address that traced back to Jamestown was actually at the Jamestown Settlement tourism site.

"There was one odd thing. Someone made a trace to the address in Tupelo about sixteen hours before we had a chance to look into the case. It's going to take some research to find out who was using an Xbox there. We have local FBI agents in both areas on their way to the locations."

"Thank you, Agent Ford."

Agent Gainer was in charge of the team that was sent to Tupelo. They arrived to find a house that was scorched inside. Upon inspection, three bodies were discovered.

Their investigation revealed that the owner of the house was a man named Steve Williams. He was presumed present, dead, and burned. Two other unidentified men were on the premises. All of the bodies would require dental records to identify them with certainty, but the driver's licenses of Steve Williams, Thomas Barlow, and Billy Monroe were on the premises. There were no female bodies. Steve's daughter, Racquel, and his wife, Amanda, were not there.

They did make a peculiar observation. There were some footprints on the burnt area. They were obviously made after the fire. They appeared to be that of someone wearing heels. Could these be the footprints of Mrs. Williams?

Regardless, someone was a step ahead of the FBI. Agent Gainer didn't like to be behind criminals. He put an all-points bulletin out on Mrs. Williams. He wasn't sure of her involvement in the murders, but tapes and DVDs discovered in the basement of the home tied her to child molestation and child pornography at a minimum.

Off in Virginia, the investigation, led by Agent Smithers, took them to the offices of the Jamestown Settlement Tourism Board. After checking every computer console and tracing hundreds of yards of cables, they were unable to find any computer or hardline drop related to the IP address of the Xbox connection. Whoever did this knew what they were doing. The next step was to run a test for a Wi-Fi connection. One was found and all the connected devices were checked out, except one. One of the devices was difficult to locate.

After a thorough search, a unique device was found above one of the drop ceiling tiles. It was a Wi-Fi device with an attached HF radio transmitter. This is something the tech guys had never seen. It was pretty high tech and appeared to be homemade or a prototype. An analysis of the device showed that it could transmit and receive radio transmissions and relay those communications to the internet via Wi-Fi and vice versa. This device was ingenious in that a number of other devices could be hooked up to it via radio waves from anywhere within twenty-five miles. That left a search area of over one thousand square miles to locate the mate or mates to this device and, if it wasn't turned on or transmitting, there was no way to locate the mate. Agent Smithers thought to himself, *This guy is absolutely brilliant. He found a way to make an untraceable internet connection.* Finding this guy wasn't going to be easy.

Three hours after the APB was put out, Mrs. Williams was found on I-55 south heading towards Jackson, Mississippi. She was taken to the Grenada, Mississippi police department. Agent Gainer headed directly there. Two hours later, he arrived at the Grenada Police Department ready to question Mrs. Williams. To his surprise, he was greeted by her lawyer who, apparently, had made the trip in less time.

"Good afternoon, Agent Gainer. I am Deborah Coleman. How are you today?"

"Miss Coleman, it is a pleasure to meet you. I am well, and you?"

"I am fine, just fine. I know you didn't expect to see me, but I am prepared to discuss terms of my client's testimony."

"Testimony? I think we have some sort of a misunderstanding. She has been taken into custody for her protection. With the gruesome discovery at her house, we think she may be a target of the individual or individuals who killed her husband and friends and we are concerned for her well-being. Is her daughter with her?"

"I am sure that you know her daughter is not here. Let's stop playing games, Agent Gainer. My client is willing to provide information about a drug ring and a child sex ring in return for entry into the witness protection program. You said you are concerned with... how did you put it...her well-being?"

"Let me make a call." Agent Gainer called his headquarters and they agreed to put her in protection if she provided credible information that brought down one major drug dealer and at least three child molesters. Agent Gainer relayed the information to Mrs. Williams' lawyer.

"Do you need to wait for the paperwork or can you trust me to talk to Mrs. Williams now?"

"I trust you, Agent Gainer."

"Before we start... If Mrs. Williams was involved in the murder of her daughter, all bets are off... Agreed?"

"If I had any inclination that she was involved in killing that little girl, I wouldn't be here. We are in agreement, Agent Gainer."

"I get it, you have standards." His sarcasm didn't go unnoticed.

Agent Gainer sat down to interview Amanda Williams. They began with Amanda's sex addiction and how it all got started for her. It turned out that she was born Amanda MacDonald from the suburbs of Chicago. One day, when Amanda was about twelve years old, her mother was suffering from a headache and her father went to the store to buy some extra strength Tylenol, which always did the trick for her mother's headaches. Shortly after taking the medication, Amanda's mother started having seizures. The seizures were unusual for her mother and she was rushed to the hospital. She died shortly after she arrived. As it turned out, Amanda's mother was one of the victims of the Tylenol cyanide poisonings. Her death was the beginning of the downfall of Amanda's life.

About four months after her mother died, her father was truly struggling with the loss of the love of his life. One night, Amanda innocently climbed into bed with her grieving father. He, in his drunkenness, almost knowingly and almost mistaking Amanda for her mother, molested her. The next morning, he was ashamed, afraid and angry with himself. That day, he went to the store and bought her the pink Huffy bike for which she had been asking before her mother had been killed. He apologized to her for what he had done and gave her the bike as a sign of his forgiveness.

But his behavior didn't change. Three days later, he climbed into her bed and committed the same atrocities with her. This time, he wasn't drunk and there was no confusion. But a gift for Amanda followed like it did before and the pattern continued until Amanda left for college at the age of eighteen.

Unfortunately, by that time, it was too late. In her mind, sex was equated to love and a way to earn things she wanted. Her behavior didn't change. She had numerous boyfriends in college, but once they were not able to provide her with lavish gifts for her "attentions," she left that boyfriend for another. The cycle of jumping from boyfriend to boyfriend continued until she met Steve Williams. He was able to provide her with not only lavish gifts, but the best drugs money could buy. Steve was the head drug dealer on campus and, with 12,000 students with hefty allowances to go with their hefty appetites for new experiences, he always had money for himself and to provide for Amanda's desires.

The two dropped out of college and married. When Steve found methamphetamines and the money they could bring him, Amanda found the incredible high they could bring her. She and Steve worked out a system where she could find competitors by posing as a woman in search of a high. Oftentimes, she would even sleep with a competitive dealer to gain his trust. She would then provide information about the dealer to Steve, who would either turn him in to the authorities anonymously or attack him. Either way, Steve would take over the competitor's turf. It was a system that kept them both satisfied. Amanda was able to fulfill her sexual and chemical "fixes" and Steve was able to grow in power and finances.

She found a marijuana dealer, Eric Creasy, who was into some "crazy shit" with sex. This guy had the best weed in town, but he and his wife loved to have sex with other people either together or separately, with each other watching or not. That all came to a stop when Eric's wife got pregnant. Oddly enough, Amanda found herself with child about six weeks later. While the two ladies were out of commission sexually, the men found some relief from the daughter of a fellow drug dealer, Thomas Barlow. When it was all said and done, the three men were trading their drugs with each other and both Eric and Steve were trading drugs for sex with Barlow's daughter, who was all of fourteen years old. Having sex with the girl and seeing how much money Barlow was making from his daughter, the two men and their wives came up with the idea to rent their children out for sex once they were of a desirable age. Through the use of their children, Amanda came across several children in the same situation. She provided their names to Agent Gainer. Additionally, she gave them "Tank" Barlow. He was Thomas's son. "I don't know his real name, but Tank took over Thomas' operation about a year ago. He supported Thomas financially with a percentage of his take every month and Thomas wasn't hurting for any cash. He could afford to rent my daughter, Racquel, on a daily basis. So he moved in with us."

Agent Gainer was quite certain that, with the coldness with which Amanda said the last two sentences, he was looking at the Devil Incarnate. *How could anyone be so completely evil?*

"Where is she now?"

"I honestly do not know. I went to the grocery store. When I returned, Steve, Barlow, and Billy were there, dead and burnt up. I looked for Racquel, but she was nowhere to be found. I don't know where that ungrateful little bitch is. She might have stolen Barlow's gun and killed them all."

Agent Gainer was now certain that he was staring at the Devil Incarnate.

"Amanda, I thank you for your time. I will let you

know how this all pans out. In the meantime, you will be kept in custody here until we can verify this information and a new identity can be set up for you. Miss Coleman, we will be in touch."

Chapter 10
A Savior is Born

Brian woke up early. Today, he could skip his run, or at least it could wait until later. For the first time in his life, he was responsible for someone other than himself. He cooked some breakfast for them all, brewed some coffee for himself, sat down to have a drink, and took a look at the morning news. There was discussion of the two houses burning and the five bodies found in Tennessee and Mississippi. The two missing children were mentioned as well. The interviews and press conferences with law enforcement officials alluded to no leads.

Brian went to wake the children. He hated to break their slumber, but he wanted to get them fed and explain everything to them. Tyler was first. "Tyler, hey bud... it's time to get up. We need to talk. There's a toothbrush in the attached bathroom. There are towels, soap, and some clothes that should fit you in there as well."

"Okay, SurfBro."

"It's Brian. SurfBro is dead."

"Okay, Brian, the artist formerly known as SurfBro."

Brian couldn't help but chuckle. It was time to wake up Rocky.

"Rocky," he said softly as he knocked on the door. "Rocky, it's time to get up. Breakfast is ready and we need to talk."

Rocky was always an early riser. The people in her old house always slept in. Waking early was the only way that she could have time to herself. When Brian stuck his head around the corner, Rocky was up and looking out the window.

"Rocky... Racquel, are you okay?"

"I don't know. Are you going to..." She paused. She needed to know the answer to a question, but she was afraid to know that answer and didn't know how to ask. "Are you going to..."

"No!" Brian interrupted forcefully but softly. "Rocky, I need to talk to both of you about who I am, where I've been, and what I've done. But I'll start with this. I was once abused like you and Tyler and I would never, ever... do anything to harm either of you."

"I'm sorry," Rocky replied.

"Sorry for what?" Brian asked.

"Sorry that you went through what we went through, and for thinking you wanted to hurt me."

"You don't have to be sorry for either. You didn't abuse me and your fear is understandable. Now, are you ready to grab some breakfast? I made pancakes."

"I L-O-V-E pancakes." She spelled out each letter.

The two met Tyler in the kitchen for breakfast.

"Okay, guys, let me tell you about who I am."

Brian went on to tell them that he, too, was abused as a child. That from the age of eleven or twelve—he really couldn't remember—he was abused by his parents. He told them how it all started with being forced to watch his parents have sex. Then he was forced to have sex with his father, "Uncle Cody," and his mother, both individually and as a group. He could see the look of shame on his mother's face and the look told him that she wasn't a willing participant.

Rocky was crying and Tyler just kept looking at the floor.

"That sounds like my parents," Tyler confessed.

He then told them about how his father slipped up with his math teacher, Coach Horton, and how "Coach H" never indicated he suspected a thing. Then one night, Coach Horton showed up at his front door with a baseball bat and a mission. He told them that Coach Horton bashed his father's face in with the bat, then did the same with Uncle Cody. He told them that "Coach H" killed them all. At the time, he didn't know the details of how it was done, but he was made aware later.

"You see, Coach Horton was abused as a child as well. He was freed by a man named Chester Tiberius Jackson.

Chester was abused as a child too. He, in turn, was freed by a man they called Romeo Brown. This 'family chain' goes on for eight generations."

"My chain is broken… Is that the chain you were talking about?" asked Tyler.

"That's the chain," Brian replied. "It's now nine generations, all the way back to the man we all refer to as Adam. He called himself that to his son. What I am about to tell you anyone can verify, in part, through Google by looking up the Blood Benders."

Brian went on to tell Tyler and Rocky the entire story of Adam.

There was no last name, just Adam. Adam was born into the Bender Family, although his birth name was not Adam. He and his family owned a small inn and general store in Labette County, Kansas. It was believed that Adam's parents were actually brother and sister, but that was rumor and conjecture. What wasn't rumor or conjecture was what his parents did for a living. From 1871 to 1873, they would lure unsuspecting well-to-do travelers to their inn, where they would rob and kill them and dispose of their bodies in the basement or elsewhere on the property. Adam was the forgotten Bender, and at eleven years old, he was much younger than his other siblings, who were in their twenties. Truth be told, his sister Kate may have been his mother or he may have been a child stolen from one of their victims.

No one knew of his existence, let alone his origins. And he couldn't recall his real name, as he was called such horrible names as "Dummy" and "Little Shit" to normal but inconsistent names such as "Johnny" and "Joseph."

In addition to the family business of robbery and murder, the family's perverse activities involved abusing Adam mentally, physically, and sexually. He survived years of abuse. It started with his siblings and, later, involved both of his parents and a few town accomplices. This abuse by his family and those accomplices went on for at least three or four years. Adam said he remembered his tenth birthday and not having been abused at that time, but that was the last birthday he remembered without abuse.

When strangers didn't come for a stay at the inn, he was abused. When they did, they were killed. Adam found himself praying for strangers to come, but that made him conflicted, as praying for their arrival meant that he wouldn't be abused, but someone would die. Finally, he just prayed for it all to end. Each and every night, he prayed to God for relief. He promised that, should he ever be freed from the abuse, he would not rest until he freed someone else. The abuse continued.

There was a doctor named William York that was investigating the disappearance of one of his neighbors, George Loncor, and his infant daughter. He went from homestead to homestead trying to gather information on his friend. Eventually, he made his way to the Bender Inn. Kate Bender, the mother, immediately jumped on him, and her husband, John Sr., killed him. They buried Doctor York along with the rest. This proved to be their undoing. Doctor York's brother was Colonel York of the United States Army. When his brother went missing, he followed his trail to investigate. Once at the Benders, they stated that Doctor York had stayed the night and moved on and that, perhaps, he might have run into some trouble with the "Savage Indians."

Colonel York felt something was amiss, but he politely agreed with the Benders and left the farm. He returned a few days later with his men and a search party. They found his brother's body and that of at least a dozen victims. The Benders were nowhere to be found, and to this day, their whereabouts are a mystery. Public information confirms this portion of the story.

What isn't in the history books is what really happened. Colonel York spotted what appeared to be his brother's scarf. Scarves weren't unique, but the pattern on the one he saw resting on a distant chair was familiar. He came back that night to spy upon the Benders and see what caused the feeling of creepiness he sensed and to see if he could figure out what the Benders were really up to. When he returned and peeked in the window, he found three of the elder Benders watching in excitement as John sexually abused the boy. He was sickened by the sight and barged into the front door and shot John Sr. in the head. He quickly dispatched the remaining three elder Benders and rescued the boy. He put the boy on his horse and he rode out to a Lakota scout and friend of his. Colonel York asked the man to take the boy out of Kansas and to the Lakota tribe to be raised as his own. The scout agreed.

Colonel York returned to the farm and made it look like the Benders had left the farm. He left the bodies uncovered in the middle of a thicket of woods miles from the Bender home to be eaten by the animals. He then returned to his unit and gathered his men to go "investigate" the Benders. The investigation revealed the remains of Doctor York and at least a dozen other victims.

Adam was raised by the chief of the tribe, Red Cloud. Red Cloud was a fierce warrior who had led the Lakota during the battle of One Hundred Slain and, later, led the Lakota in settling for peace under the Treaty of Fort Laramie. Adam would still see Colonel York from time to time, but the young man and the officer would never acknowledge each other's presence.

Adam's arrival in the Lakota camp was not a happy moment in time. Although he was happy to have been freed from his less than miserable existence by Colonel York, he was thrown into a culture that was beyond anything he understood. Few of the people spoke English and he certainly didn't speak Lakota. The clothing those around him wore bore little resemblance to what he was accustomed.

Although it was made clear to all members of the tribe that Adam was to be treated as Chief Red Cloud's son and no adult would defy his orders, the children saw him as different and treated him as such as they knew whatever punishment they would receive would be minimal. They picked on him because of his short hair and pale skin. They taunted him because they knew there was no fight in him, both in desire and in know-how. From day one, the taunting started. Anytime Adam was away from Chief Red Cloud, the kids would taunt him. This taunting continued for months.

One of the children that was a constant pest to Adam

was Little Wolf. He was the son of Grey Wolf, one of Red Cloud's most trusted and fierce warriors. Little Wolf wanted to be the man his father was, but he was spoiled and lived by his father's reputation and not by any deeds or accomplishments of his own. In fact, he relied on his father's reputation and accomplishments so much that he neglected his training and practice and was nowhere as skilled as a warrior as the other boys his age, but that was still far superior to Adam.

Little Wolf's favorite thing to do to Adam was to wrestle him to the ground and choke him. When Adam would open his mouth in an attempt to catch a breath of air, Little Wolf would spit in his mouth. The other boys would laugh. Then Little Wolf would get up and proclaim in Lakota, "I am Little Wolf, son of the great warrior Grey Wolf. I too am a great warrior and this pale face is as useless as buffalo shit." Little Wolf would then turn his back to Adam, showing the ultimate disrespect, and walk away.

Each time, Adam would lie there on the ground with his head to the side, continuously spitting, all the while crying. After a few minutes, he would get up and run away.

What the other boys didn't know was that Adam would run to Grey Wolf, careful to show up after all of the crying had ceased and the evidence of the attack had waned from his face. Once there, he would ask Grey Wolf to help train him as a warrior. Grey Wolf, being obedient to Red Cloud and always eager to train another warrior, would oblige. Grey Wolf taught Adam, who he called White Calf, because he saw the strength of a buffalo in him.

Unbeknownst to the other boys, Grey Wolf saw and knew of every encounter and he saw the great resolve and strength in this young pale-faced child. He took great pleasure in helping to turn him into a warrior. They would go over arts of hand-to-hand combat and the Lakota version of judo and he would teach White Calf to shoot an arrow and how to use a tomahawk to disable and eventually kill his opponent.

Finally, after over four months of abuse and subsequent training, Adam had had enough. The change from victim to victor was so quick, the children in observance along with Little Wolf were left in a state of shock. As Little Wolf made the start of his daily attack by shoving Adam, Adam grabbed Little Wolf's arms and fell backwards while simultaneously raising his knees, and as his back hit the ground, he used his legs to throw Little Wolf over his head. Little Wolf landed hard on his back. In fact, he hit the ground hard enough to knock the wind out of his lungs.

Adam quickly scampered on top of Little Wolf, and as Little Wolf gasped for air, Adam sucked in all the phlegm and snot he could muster, but he spat to the side Little Wolf's head, although he could have easily dripped the mucus into Little Wolf's mouth. Then he stood and proclaimed in perfect Lakota, "I am White Calf, adopted son of Red Cloud and I, too, will one day be a great warrior and, hopefully... (he paused for several seconds) Little Wolf will fight by my side." After his proclamation, he stood up and offered Little Wolf his hand. Little Wolf took it and White Calf helped him up. Adam had sense enough to know that making an enemy out of Little Wolf might be satisfying in the short run, but over the years, having such an enemy would not be wise. The two young men embraced as brothers and the rest of the young men cheered them on.

From that day forward, Adam focused on becoming a warrior and learning all he could from his adopted father and his "uncle" Grey Wolf. Over the years, he perfected his use of the traditional tools of the Lakota, the tomahawk, the spear, the bow and others. He learned to speak the language of his new family fluently and he learned to track game. And he managed to do all of this while staying out of sight and remaining unknown to the Indian Agents that patrolled the area.

When he reached the age of a man, he walked away from the tribe with Chief Red Cloud's blessing. The day he left, he began his quest to find another victim to save.

He searched for years to find a victim. It wasn't easy. There was no internet back in those days; no television and no radio. There simply was not the information that there is today. One day, he came across one of those that had abused him. Adam was now a grown man at the age of twenty-one, he believed. The man didn't recognize Adam, as he was just another piece of meat to the man, but Adam didn't forget any of the faces of those that had abused him, especially this man with the scar across his face, which went from just above his left eye straight down his cheek. The damage from the injury that caused the scar also left him with a discolored left eye.

He stalked the man like he would a deer. He tracked him to his home, a cabin on the outside edge of town. At night, he looked in one of the two cabin windows and saw that the man had a family. He had a wife and a son.

Adam was not on a quest for revenge. That was not the deal he made with God. But once he saw the man move to his own child's bed and begin to abuse him with the mother watching, he knew he had found a victim to rescue. He used all his training as a Lakota warrior to make his attack.

He looked at the door of the cabin and realized the hinges were on the left side of the door and the door opened to the outside. He moved to that side of the door. It would provide cover for him once the door was opened. He created a diversion by throwing a nearby rock against the cabin to the right of the door frame. The man yelled out, "Who's out there?"

Adam threw another rock. This time, the door burst open and the man exited with his Winchester rifle in hand. Adam quickly used his tomahawk to knock the man out. Next, he quickly moved to the woman and did the same. The boy cowered in the corner between the wall and the bed. Adam rushed to the boy before he could scream and put a hand over his mouth. "I am not here to hurt you, son. No one will hurt you anymore." He grabbed the boy and took him into the woods about one hundred yards from the cabin. There, he led him into a small tent and gave him a buffalo hide blanket to keep warm.

"Young man, I am here to free you from this way of life. I promise you that I will never do the things to you that these people have done. I am offering you a chance at a life without abuse. It is your choice to accept this life or not. I am going to go inside and make sure these people never hurt anyone ever again. If you want to come with me, then stay here safe and warm until I return. If not, go wherever you want to go. I will not follow or track you, but I will move on with my life without you. This is your choice," Adam told the boy in a calm and assuring tone.

Adam turned to walk away. As he walked away, the boy asked, "What's your name?"

"If you are here when I return, I will tell you my name and everything about me."

Adam quickly returned to the cabin, dragged the man into the house, and tied him to a chair using the man's own lasso from the saddle that was stationed just inside the door. He tied the woman's arms and legs to the four posts of the bed. He muffled both just as he had done with the boy. He walked out to the water trough and took a scoop of water. He threw it on the woman's face and she awoke. He did the same with the man.

As the man started to regain consciousness, Adam smashed his left knee with his tomahawk. The man let out a muffled scream.

He went back to the woman, took out a knife and cut across the woman's arm. The cut was deep but not life threatening. The woman tried to scream. The muffle kept the sound low.

The man tried to squirm out of the ties and yelled out, but his yells were still muffled.

"Your actions and her inaction have brought the wrath of God upon you."

With that, he smashed the man's right knee just as he did the left. Again, this resulted in muffled screams.

Then Adam cut the woman's other arm. She screamed again. The sorry excuse of a father screamed more. Both were still muffled. Adam used his knife to cut the man from knee to groin. He grabbed the nearby kerosene lamp. He poured some of the fluid over each of the parents' heads and lit them on fire. He put the flame out with a blanket and left the abusers there to suffer until they died.

He went out to the boy and told him, "I went through

the same thing you went through. My parents did to me what your parents did to you. You will never go through that again. If you want me to, I will take you to live with me and no one will ever hurt you again. If not, I'll leave you here and disappear."

The boy agreed to go with Adam and he took the child to safety back on the Pine Ridge Reservation. There, he raised that child as his own and in the traditions of the Lakota Band of the Sioux Nation. He told him that the only thing he had to do to repay him was to "pay it forward" by saving another abused child.

"Eventually, he did and that tradition was what has been passed down to me rescuing you two," Brian finished.

Chapter 11
The Training Begins

"My duty was to rescue one; that was you, Tyler. But, this guy," Brian pointed to Tyler, "would not quit until I rescued you, Rocky. That's why there are three of us at this table and not two."

"So are you saying we have to rescue someone else?" Tyler asked.

"What I am saying is this. If you are willing, I will raise the two of you as my own children. I will not touch or abuse you in the ways that you have known. I will train you in the ways that I have been trained, which have evolved from the Lakota training of Adam. I will teach you all the things that I have learned and I will leave it up to you as to whether or not you will rescue someone else. To be honest, none of us down the line have been able to NOT rescue another."

"I'm in," Rocky replied. "I always saw myself as some sort of trained ninja, kind of like Natasha on the *Avengers*."

"I guess I'm in too," Tyler said with uncertainty.

"Tyler, all I need to know from you today is... Do you want to live with me and have me be your new father? The rest is not important right now."

"I'm definitely down with that," Tyler affirmed.

"The most important rule that I have is that you do not question me or ask why we are doing anything. Everything we will do will be to aid in your recovery and prepare you for the future. The first thing we have to do is to get an identity for Rocky. I planned for you, Tyler. I have an identity and clothes. Everything is in place for you. Rocky, it will take some time for me to get an identity for you. We'll also have to get some clothes for you. Most importantly, I have to make sure the FBI is not on our tail. Tyler, do you still have that number?"

"I do."

"Put that somewhere that you will never lose it... in your head. I want you to memorize it. You should know that number better than your birthday. Rocky, you need to memorize it too."

"Whose phone number is it?" Racquel asked.

"It's Coach Horton's. Let's be clear. Coach Horton is not responsible for you. I am. But if anything were to ever happen to me, call him. He will take care of you. The next thing you two need to know is where you can get money. Again, if anything ever happens to me, all the money you will need to get to 'Coach H' is right here."

Brian went to the fireplace, pulled out the logs and the grate, and lifted a few bricks under the grate. There, he removed a metal box filled with $5,000 in twenty-dollar bills.

"This is not for a new outfit, tennis shoes, or Xbox games. This is getaway or survival cash. There's more at three other places near here. I'll show you as time goes on. This is the easiest one to get, but if the house is blocked or you can't get back to it, the other spots will help.

"Are we straight on the money and Coach H?"

"Yes, sir!" Racquel replied with a salute. This caused both Brian and Tyler to chuckle.

"Next, I want you to understand two things. First of all, everything that has happened to you up until now is NOT YOUR FAULT!" Brian stressed those last three words. "It wasn't my fault that it happened to me. It wasn't Coach Horton's fault that it happened to him. It wasn't Adam's fault that he was abused by his parents. What has happened to us is the fault of the sick people that we were born to. God trusted them to raise us and their duty was to protect us, not do the sick things to us that they did. I want you to put all of that behind you. That will be difficult to do. Trust me, I know. But, one day, you will wake up and the fear of someone violating you won't be the first thought of your day. You will be able to trust a few people close to you and trust that they won't hurt you. You will be able to go on to have a somewhat normal life."

"Somewhat normal?" questioned Rocky.

"Somewhat. Because when you're older, you will be thinking about making your own rescue, how to find him or her and how to make the rescue."

"No. That doesn't sound exactly normal," Tyler replied.

"Second, you two are now brother and sister. Whether you want to be intimate with each other or not, you cannot anymore. This will help with you recovering from all that has happened. Got it?"

"I don't want him; he's too short."

"She's too skinny."

"Seriously, Brian. We are friends. We were forced to do the things we did. In all that craziness and gross stuff, we found each other as friends and talked to each other about what was happening to us. We didn't want to be together like that then and we don't want to now."

"Or ever," Racquel added.

"Then we are all on the same page. Today, your training in the ways of the Lakota begins. Starting today, what you will learn will help you in the future whether you decide to rescue another victim or not. Go change your clothes and get some athletic gear on. Boots or sneakers will be best for shoes. We are going on a little run."

Brian knew he needed to check to see if he left any tracks or bread crumbs for the FBI to follow, but he needed his run to get a clear mind and get himself set for the rest of the day's activities. He also knew he needed to lighten the mood a touch.

"Do you want to hear a quick story about the first time I visited my grandfather in this very cabin?" he asked.

"Sure!" Tyler and Rocky replied in unison.

"When I first visited this cabin, it was smaller and all that was here was my grandfather, two beds, and cold water. When I walked in the door, my grandfather asked me if I wanted a sandwich. I told him I did. He served it to me on a plate that didn't appear to be totally clean. When I asked him about it, he said to me, 'That's the best cold water can do.' I really didn't think too much about it. Later that evening, he made his famous chili. I grabbed a bowl when he was ready to serve it to me, but that bowl and all of the rest didn't seem to be totally clean either. Again, I brought it to his attention. Again, he told me, 'That's the best cold water can do' and I just ate chili out of the bowl. Not long after I finished eating, I heard a scratching at the door. My grandfather got up and went to the door and let a dog in. The dog came up to me and I petted him. I asked what his name was and, as my grandfather placed his bowl on the ground and the dog walked over to it and started licking the bowl, he said, 'I told you… his name is Cold Water.'"

"Eww," Rocky replied as Tyler let out a belly-filled laugh. Both Brian and Rocky started laughing as well.

Chapter 12
Tracing the Untraceable

The Cyber Crimes Division had its hands full trying to track the phantom connection. They recovered the transmittal device and analyzed it. They found that it worked similarly to the Navy's Link 11 system. It used HF and UHF radio to transmit data. It was very much like the Wi-Fi in most homes or offices. The only difference was the HF and UHF frequencies moved the range from a Wi-Fi's range of about one hundred feet to twenty-five miles or more. The only way to find out who was broadcasting was to search for someone broadcasting on a similar frequency. The difficulty lay in the fact that any HAM radio operator broadcasted in the same frequency range. Even CB radios found in nearly every tractor trailer were on the upper end of this range. This device had a specialized receiver at 5 MHz that received an encrypted signal, causing it to tune the data transmitter and receiver to another frequency within the HF range. Without deciphering the encryption and receiving the broadcast, there was no way to know what frequency to attempt to trace. The FBI needed to get the device back in place and hope to intercept the broadcasts.

Agents in Tupelo recovered the Xbox there, and as suspected, they were able to connect this device to the internet connection at the Creasys'. They found no Jamestown connection to this Xbox.

Chief Caldwell was working on the molestation angle. He sent the DVDs to the FBI for some facial recognition of the participants. They were able to find three people that were in a vast majority of the videos other than Eric Creasy. The Bureau gave Chief Caldwell their names and addresses. Unfortunately for Chief Caldwell's investigation, two of the men were the "crispy critters" in Tupelo, which was unfortunate for the men as well. It seems that there was some sort of a *quid pro quo* between the two fathers. Steve Williams and Billy Monroe were not going to give Chief Caldwell any information. The third suspected molester was a man named Bruce Goring. He lived in Memphis, Tennessee not more than thirty minutes from Chief Caldwell's town. He needed the cooperation of the Memphis City Police. A quick call to his buddy Chief Ernest Wall had him on the case. Chief Wall would locate Mr. Goring and bring him in for questioning.

Chief Wall gave his buddy, Chris, a call the next day to let him know they had Goring in custody and he was free to speak to the suspected monster. They agreed on a meeting an hour from the call.

"Hello, Mr. Goring. I am Chief Caldwell of the Mannford Police Department. How are you doing today? Is there anything I can get you? A cup of coffee?"

"I'm shitty because I am sitting in a police station with all of these dirtbags being questioned by the likes of you. You can get me the hell out of here, and no, I don't want any of your damn coffee."

Chief Caldwell didn't expect this to be easy, but he was taken aback by Bruce Goring's hostility.

He pulled a picture out of the file in front of him. This picture was a freeze frame from one of the videos but showed none of the molestation. It was simply a picture of the three men together.

"Tell me what you know about Steve Williams and Billy Monroe."

"I don't know shit. Who are Steve Washington and Billy Madison?"

His attempt to show confusion amused Chief Caldwell.

"Okay, I am going to be straight with you. Hopefully, you'll be straight with me. Because if you're not, I can't help you and, one way or another, you are going to need my help."

"I don't need shit from the likes of you or your kind."

Chief Caldwell pulled out two more pictures. These were pictures of the Crispy Critters formerly known as Steve Williams and Billy Monroe.

"This is Steve Williams," Chief stated as he pulled out the first picture. "And this is Billy Monroe. They are known acquaintances of Eric Creasy." Next, he pulled out a picture of Eric Creasy's charred remains. "And this is Eric. Someone is going around killing your friends. He is instituting a scorched earth policy and I don't mean that figuratively. Frankly, I think he's doing us and the world a favor, but my job is 'to serve and protect' and there is no stipulation on who I protect. I have over thirty-five DVDs from the Creasy house that show you participating in child molestation along with these three dead men and with several other men and women. So, I am asking you again, what can you tell me about Steve Williams, Billy Monroe, and Eric Creasy?"

"I want a lawyer and immunity. Once I get that, I will tell you all that I know."

"Chief Wall, can you get the District Attorney here and see if we can work something out?"

A discussion between the D.A. and the two chiefs led to a compromise where he would have immunity from everything seen on the DVDs at the Creasy house. What Chief Caldwell and the D.A. didn't let Bruce Goring know was that the FBI had matched his face to some pending internet molestation cases they had on file. So letting him walk on the cases from the Creasy house wasn't going to keep Bruce Goring out of prison and being the victim of prison justice.

Forty-five minutes after Chief Wall walked out of the interview to talk to the D.A., he re-entered the interrogation room with a signed immunity agreement from the district attorney. "Here you go, Mr. Goring. As agreed, you are immune from prosecution from anything related to what we have regarding the DVDs. Once you sign the agreement, you are clear to walk out of here. However, this agreement is null and void should you not provide information regarding the individuals involved and the circumstances regarding these cases."

Bruce Goring was so excited about not being prosecuted for the crimes the police talked to him about, he didn't think about the stuff that he had done that the police hadn't discussed and he assumed they didn't know about.

Also, he was in such a hurry to be "free" of what would happen to him in prison had he been convicted that he signed the document without hesitation and without waiting for his lawyer to arrive. That was exactly what Chief Caldwell had hoped for.

Bruce then told them about the operation; how participants found the "pods," as they called them, and how the "pods" found participants. He gave the names of all the men and women in the DVDs, or at least the names by which they were known. This gave Chief Caldwell and the observing FBI agents leads to continue the investigation. At the very least, they could break up the local "pods" and the FBI had new intelligence on how to find "pods" using similar methods.

Bruce walked out of the police station a free man, just as Chief Caldwell promised. However, he didn't walk far; waiting outside the station was the local Bureau's Agent in Charge of the case. He arrested Bruce on the spot for the crimes he had committed not on the DVDs, but those which the FBI had evidence of from their internet files.

"Do you think one of their own turned on Eric, Steve, and the others?" Chief Wall asked his buddy Chris.

"I'm not sure," Chris replied.

Chief Caldwell returned to his office with a list of eight names, four of which were local, according to Bruce. He needed to get the addresses and warrants to search their homes for additional information.

Once back at the office, Chief Caldwell did a search for the names supplied by Bruce Goring. He was able to come up with four local addresses, just like Bruce said. The other four were out of state as far away as Seattle, Washington. He spoke to Agent Rigby and she agreed to track down those leads with the local field offices. One way or another, those sickos would be off of the streets in short order.

As Chief picked up the phone to call the local judge to get search warrants on the four, Reggie walked in. "Hey, Chief, you got a minute?" Chief Caldwell hung up the phone.

"What's up?"

"I was doing some research on the Creasy killings, and

when that stuff happened in Tupelo, I started looking for similar cases."

"And..."

"I found something strange. I found a bunch of arsons resulting in charred remains in the houses. Those happen nearly every day. Then I narrowed the search to people tied up and victims of arson. That field got smaller, but there were still a ton."

"I could have told you that. Most of the time when someone wants to cover their tracks, they burn down the evidence."

"Yeah, but then I looked for cut-up and tied-up victims and arson and I got to a small group. When I started looking into these cases and added a kidnapped or missing child, the field got really small."

"How small?"

"Going back twenty years, there are fifteen such cases and, in twelve of them, the children were found. Most of these were one parent trying to get custody of their kid, ugly divorces, etc. However, right around thirteen years ago, there were three cases in which a child was never recovered and there was no known motive. In case number one, there were three bodies found, two men and one woman and one boy was missing and never found. One of the men had his genitals mutilated, apparently by a knife. Kind of like our man Eric Creasy and the shotgun blast and the gash running up his leg. In the other two cases, there were similar mutilations inflicted on the parents and the children were missing, both boys."

"That is crazy. Do you have any case files?"

"I contacted the police department in Fayetteville, NC and they were able to send me a preliminary report of the first case via email. They are overnighting the rest, but here is what they gave me."

Sure enough, the report showed two dead men, one cut from his knee to his groin and through his testicles; the other had his genitals split. The woman was killed, mercifully, by slitting her throat. All of the bodies were burned.

"Wow, this is eerily similar to our case. What about the other two?"

"I have calls in to the departments where the cases occurred, but I am awaiting call-backs."

"Let me know what you find out."

"That's not all."

"What do you mean?"

"I found another group of four cases from about fifteen years before the first group of cases with the same MO. They all happened within an eighteen-month period from 1957 to 1959. In each case, a man and woman were killed. In one case, the man was sliced from knee to groin and through the scrotum; both bodies were burned and the kid was MIA. The other three had similar mutilations inflicted on men with a dead wife and missing sons."

"Are you telling me we have a serial killer on our hands dating back forty years?"

"No, I am telling you I have three different groups of cases similar to ours dating back some sixty-plus years."

"Three groups of cases?"

"Yes, I found a third group of cases. One of the cases, from Los Angeles, had a man with a cut groin, a dead wife, and a missing child. Both parents' bodies were burned and a son was never found. There were two more cases during the same period with similar mutilations. They all occurred during a period between 1947 to 1950. I don't have all the details on these because of their age, but they sound eerily similar to our case and the other groups of cases.

"I called the Los Angeles Police Department about the one case. They were able to look into their records and gave me the groin and genitals piece. Here's the kicker... The dead man was suspected of sexually abusing his child, but the investigation ended once he was found dead."

"So you are telling me that an eighty-year-old man at the youngest has been going around and killing people in this manner every fifteen years or so since as early as 1947?"

"Boss, you always told me not to jump to conclusions but to use my instincts. I am telling you that there are at least four groups of murder cases, including ours, that are very similar dating back to 1947. If one man committed these murders, he'd be in his eighties at the youngest, assuming he was twenty to twenty-five years old when it all started."

The amazement on Chief Caldwell's face couldn't be hidden. "Do you know of an eighty-year-old man that can overpower a forty-year-old man the size of Eric Creasy, string up his wife, pull her to the ceiling, and do the job that the assailant did at the Creasy house? If such a man exists, he shouldn't be too hard to find."

"Contact Agent Rigby. Tell her about your discovery and see if the FBI kidnapping unit can give you any other similar cases and any more detail on the four you have. They have been in charge of kidnapping cases since 1932. They should have the records on every kidnapping case since. Hell, maybe even before. I was just getting ready to call Judge Martinez to get warrants on these four scumbags. In fact, I may have hung up on her when you walked in. Man, this case gets crazier by the minute."

"You got that right, Chief. This case is crazy. I'll give Agent Rigby a call."

Chapter 13
A Better Idea

When Brian and the two children returned from their run, there was a message on Brian's actual cell phone. That reminded him to kill the burner phone. When he saw he had a missed call, he looked to see who had called him. As he had feared, it was work calling. Here he was in day five of his two-week vacation and work was calling. The last time, it only took them two days, so he imagined this was an improvement.

"Agent Smart, this is Agent Ford." Agent Ford didn't have to say who he was. Brian worked with him every day. He knew his voice better than he knew most. "I need you to give me a call right away. We have kind of an urgent matter and odd situation regarding an HF transmitter and the internet. We were hoping you could help us do some tracking."

Damn, they must have found my Jamestown connection. This was bad news, but not that bad. It was good news at the same time. He'd made that device and knew there was no way to trace it unless he broadcast to it. Knowing the FBI was listening meant that he wouldn't be transmitting, at least not to that device. The bad news was that he would have to be more careful using his other devices. If they knew how to track the frequency he was using, they might be able to detect his other devices. He would have to use them sparingly and only for things he didn't want traced back to him. That meant he'd better hurry and set up Rocky's identity. For that, he could use the device installed at the local library's system. They were over three hundred miles away from Jamestown. No one would be tracking that far away and, apparently, they didn't have the know-how. That was why they were calling him.

He would call the office first, use his standard satellite

connection to do whatever work they wanted from him, and then he'd get Rocky a new identity.

"Rocky, Tyler, I need you guys quiet. You can go outside, go get showers; whatever. I need to call my job and the sound of children in the background is going to be a little difficult to explain."

"Got it," replied Tyler.

"Church mice," replied Rocky.

Brian called Agent Ford. He was given an explanation about the situation, the murders and burned bodies, the DVDs found at the Creasy house, the Xbox connection leading them to Tupelo where more bodies were found, and the point of the phone call, the device in Jamestown.

Brian asked for pictures of the device, its circuit boards, its antennae, etc. "Boss, did you get any broadcasts to or from the device?" He knew the answer but had to ask to cover his tracks.

"No, Agent Smart, we haven't. Look, I know you're on vacation, but this is big. I need you on this. I know you can't get back here right away, but I need you to consult. Agent Caruso is working the specs and might have some information. Let me transfer you to him and you two see what you can come up with."

"I understand, boss. I'll talk to Larry and we'll see what we can come up with. Is it okay if he gives you our findings or do you want something from me?"

"Agent Caruso can fill me in. Thanks for doing this, Brian. I owe you."

"No need to thank me. I haven't done anything yet."

Brian talked to Larry and it seemed that Larry and the tech guys had a good handle on the device and how it worked. No prints were found on it. He had made sure of that. None of the components were traceable. Of course, he had ensured that as well. After a quick view of the circuit board and the antenna, Brian threw them a bone. "Larry, from what I can see given the configuration, this thing receives a signal, probably in the lower HF range. Once that is received, it switches to another frequency, probably set by the transmitter of the offsite device. The new frequency is used to receive and it appears to transmit on another frequency. My guess is plus or minus 100 Hz from the receive frequency." He knew the differences in the two channels was exactly 100 minus 18.73 Hz so 81.17 Hz from the initial frequency. He picked that number because that was the year that Adam was freed.

"We figured on about 5 Hz for the setup, but we didn't catch the 100 Hz difference. Thanks, man. Any idea how to catch this guy?"

"I would monitor the lower band, say 1 to 10 Hz for a transmission, and if that thing turns on, then you know what he is using for a starting frequency. The next step would be to try to trace the frequency coming out of the device. That's going to be harder. I'd set up an antenna at the device and four more surrounding it a mile or so. Once it's on, tune those receivers to the frequency the device is broadcasting on plus or minus 100 Hz. You should be able to triangulate from there. It is all going to depend on him turning on the device and keeping it on for a good while, though. How long was it down?"

"Four hours."

"Hopefully, he didn't notice."

"Yeah, I hope so. Thanks again, man. Enjoy the rest of your vacation."

"Will do. Let me know if you need more."

The news was better than he'd thought. They had no clue who was attached to the relay device. Now it was time to find an identity for Rocky. Normally, the first step was to find a female near her age with the same first name that was deceased. He didn't want hiccups with the children by changing their names. This was a lesson learned way down the line of Adam's family. Children had a habit responding to their given name and it was much easier to change their last name and keep their first name to avoid mistakes. He only needed a name and a date of birth. He also needed someone without a social security number. Say, for instance, he found a Racquel Martin, he could apply for a social security card with that name and date of birth. This way, he could create a person in "the system" under the name Racquel Martin. This is a form of identity theft called "ghosting." And with Brian's programming expertise, he could tap into the Social Security Administration and make Racquel Martin alive again. Then he could either give Rocky the old Racquel Martin's social security number, if she had one, or create a new one. This was how it was done for him, this was how he did it for Tyler, and this was how it would work for Rocky. An easy fix for Rocky came in the form of Tyler's identity.

Tyler assumed the identity of Tyler Summers, a boy that was killed in a car accident along with his entire family, including his younger sister, Ann Summers. Ann had no middle name but with a few strokes from Brian's keyboard, it became Racquel. Today, Ann would be thirteen. Rocky had just aged a year. Next, he hacked into the Social Security Administration's database, erased Ann Summer's date of death, and activated her inoperative social security number. He then hacked into Portland, Oregon's school database and created transcripts in the name of Ann Racquel Summers. Tyler and Rocky would be brother and sister. This would make it easier for all of them to blend in.

An hour and a half after Brian started, Racquel Williams was Ann "Racquel" Summers. She was a B average student after having waited a year to enroll in kindergarten because of the deaths of her parents. Losing a year of school would allow her to maintain her actual grade level at school. The children would be enrolled in a home school and online combination program through the local school district. This would allow Brian to devote half of their days to training and the other half to education. For the first year or so, they would have regular but limited contact with the local community. Basically, they would ease into their new names and roles over that first year. By then, they should be ready to reenter society under their assumed identities.

In order to complete the team, Brian would have to resign his position with the FBI. This was going to be difficult for him because he really enjoyed working with his team and felt he was making a difference at his job. He hoped that he could be hired as a part-time consultant. That could wait until his vacation was nearly over. In the meantime, it was back to training the next generation of "The Family" and monitoring the situation with the investigation.

"Rocky and Tyler, I need to talk to you. Here is how this is going to work. You two did very well on the run this morning. Running a mile in ten minutes is respectable. Over the next few months, we are going to increase the distance and make your times faster. I want you to be able to run five miles in under forty minutes by the end of the year."

"Five miles. That's crazy. Why would anyone want to run five miles?" asked Tyler.

Brian remained calm. "Tyler, I will explain myself this one time. Remember our deal. You do as I say. No questions. There is a reason behind everything that we do in 'The Family.' Running does a number of things. It helps your endurance, which may be needed in a fight or should you need to flee from a situation. It allows you to clear your head. You will learn that running is a form of meditation. Running burns calories and will help you not to get fat, slow, or sluggish.

"So here's the good news. No school next year." The children smiled with that statement. "You guys are going to take it slow in becoming your new selves. Tyler, you are now Tyler Summers, and Rocky, you are now Ann Racquel Summers. We can still call you 'Rocky.' As you may have guessed, you are brother and sister. Your parents died in a car accident and I am your uncle Brian. We will complete your schooling at home and with some online courses. Sound good?"

"What about sports?" Tyler asked.

"Tyler, you are going to have to take a year off. After we complete the next school year, we'll get you guys into high school and you can participate then, okay?"

"Okay."

"Tomorrow, we are up early. We have to make a trip into town to get some clothes for Rocky. The next day, we are going to start to learn to hunt."

"Uncle Brian," Rocky started, "can I ask you a question, not about running or anything like that?"

"Sure."

"If there are other kids out there like us, shouldn't we rescue them as well? Why would we let them suffer and only save one victim ten or fifteen years from now?"

"I... That's a good question, Rocky. Can I think about it for a while and get back to you?"

"Of course."

Brian's mind was spinning. It had been so ingrained in him to save one that he never contemplated saving another. Couldn't he save more? Why did "The Way" only involve saving one?

Chapter 14
A Long History

Chief Caldwell found it easy to track down the four "gentlemen" in question named by Bruce Goring. The first was Michael James. Once they entered Mr. James' residence, it was apparent that he had nothing to do with the deaths. Mr. James had cerebral palsy and had very little use of his legs. This caused him to walk with crutches. He even used a motorized wheelchair while at home. There was no way for him to have committed the murders; however, that did not absolve him of the molestation. A quick search of his computer revealed videos of him with an apparently young girl. Additionally, investigators found various videos of children being molested by other men and pornography involving children on the computer's hard drive. He was arrested on the spot and charged with several counts of child molestation and child pornography.

Next on the list was a woman named Karen Stevenson. She was not as easy to rule out as a murder suspect. She was large in stature, standing over six feet tall. Once in the house, it became very apparent that she was a bodybuilder. She had pictures of herself from competitions on her walls. Her kitchen was full of powdered supplements, fruits and vegetables, and a blender. She appeared to be someone that was more concerned with staying in shape than molesting children, but a search of her computer proved differently. She had videos of her with both young boys and girls. The tech team also found emails from someone that appeared to be her father apologizing for the things he had done to her and her brother. They found emails from her brother, Thomas, discussing his impulses and trying not to act on them and how his head was messed up by the things their dad made them do. It was obvious that this woman was a victim of sexual abuse from a young age and, as is often the case, abuse begat abuse. She was arrested and charged with several counts of child molestation and child pornography.

While on his way to the third location, Chief Caldwell received a call from Reggie. "Hey, Chief, the FBI just got back to me. We found one more matching case."

"Recent?" Chris asked.

"Only if you count 1937 as recent. Our serial killer just turned ninety-five. I ran our theory by the FBI and they aren't buying the serial killer angle. I thought it was farfetched with an eighty-year-old assailant myself, but ninety-five is totally out of the question. I have another idea, though."

"Copycats?"

"Not exactly. When you are done with the next guy, can we sit down for a talk? I want to run this scenario by you."

"Sure thing, Reggie. I'll give you a call when I'm heading back to the office."

The third suspect was Zachary Johnson. He was a high school dropout and known member of the People's Alliance for a Colorless America, which proclaimed itself to be a civil rights group. In this case, "colorless" meant purely white. Once at the house, the police were met with shotgun fire from the kitchen window. Zach had somehow been alerted and he wasn't going without a fight. *A fight would make the D.A.'s job a bit easier*, thought Chief Caldwell. He had his men pull back and stationed Deputy Childress one hundred yards up the hill with his "sniper rifle." His "sniper rifle" was his personal hunting rifle, a .308 bolt-action rifle with a high-powered scope. Trent had been shooting this gun or one very similar to it since he was thirteen years old. He could hit soda cans easily at three hundred yards or more. He set himself up on the roof of his police SUV, set up the gun's bipod, assumed a semi-prone position, and trained his rifle on Zach's kitchen window.

Chief Caldwell suited up in his riot gear, which included a helmet and a Kevlar vest. He drove towards Zach's trailer and spoke on his car's loudspeaker as he approached.

"Zach Johnson, I am coming out of my car unarmed. Do not shoot or you will be fired upon."

He positioned the car in such a manner that the driver's side was away from the trailer. As he began to step out of the car, shotgun pellets exploded the passenger side window. Even in the chaos, Chris was able to hear the pump of the shotgun as Zach chambered another round. He was pinned down and the only option he had was to hide behind the car. Before he was able to move, he heard a kitchen window shatter and then came the familiar sound of the .308 being fired from a distance. The People's Alliance for a Colorless America and the Creasy pod were both one member smaller. Deputy Childress' bullet found its target, the heart. Zachary Johnson was dead before anyone could get to him and check for a pulse.

This was going to be a mess to clean up and the paperwork was going to be a royal pain in the ass, but Trent's shot was warranted and clean. There would be no need for him to be "suspended with pay pending an investigation." Once the coroner and forensics team was done with their part, the tech team was able to extract large amounts of child pornography from his computer and a number of videos of Mr. Johnson molesting children. Chief Caldwell was glad this worthless member of society was no longer on the streets, but he believed a bullet didn't allow for his deserved suffering and he was correct: the D.A.'s job had gotten easier.

When Chief Caldwell arrived back at the office, Reggie was there to meet him.

"Chief, are you okay?"

"Yeah, I'm good, Reggie. Caught a piece of the passenger window in my hand. It's really just a scratch, nothing to worry about."

"I know your plate is full; do you want to wait and try this tomorrow?"

"No, I think hearing your theory will make my day better. Give me some time to debrief Trent and make sure that he's okay. Killing a man is no easy task."

"Chief, have you ever?" His hesitant question was interrupted.

"Yeah, Reggie, I have, but let's not talk about that

now. I need to talk to Deputy Childress. Give me about fifteen minutes. Then I'll hear your theory."

Chief Caldwell summoned Deputy Childress to his office and closed the door behind him. Uncharacteristically, he closed the blinds to his office window.

"Have a seat, Trent."

"Thanks, Chief."

"Trent, I think you've earned the right to call me Chris. Let me first say, 'Thank you.' Thank you for saving my life. There is very little doubt that, because of you, I am here to have this conversation with you. I am thankful and, although she stands to gain substantially from my life insurance policy, I am certain Mrs. Caldwell thanks you."

The two men chuckled at that for a few seconds. Then, perhaps because of the magnitude of the situation, outright laughed harder than the joke deserved for a good bit. When the laughing stopped, Chief Caldwell asked, "Seriously, Trent, are you okay?"

"I'm fine."

"Look, I know that taking a man's life is never easy and I know that from experience. So, let me ask you once again. Are you okay?"

"Honestly, Chie…" Chief Caldwell gave Trent a look of disapproval.

"Honestly, Chris…" Trent accentuated the word Chris. "…I am." He paused for a few seconds and appeared to be in deep thought. Then he continued, "You know the last day of deer-hunting season, I was sitting up in my tree stand and this beautiful 'twelve-point' walked out about the same distance as the shot I took today. At first, I was reluctant to shoot the fella because he was so beautiful and you know I hunt for food, not trophies. But after a few moments, I realized how much deer chili, sausage, and venison steaks a buck this size could make. I took my aim right at his heart and lungs, and just as I squeezed the trigger, something caught his attention and he turned just enough for my shot to miss the lethal zone and the bullet struck him in the gut. He didn't drop. Instead, he bolted. I tracked that deer for two miles through brush, sticker bushes, muck, and God knows what else and, when I finally found him lying on the ground, he was still alive. He was letting out this God-awful moan. That sound sickened me. Without hesitation, I took out my service pistol and shot him in the head to put him out of his misery. Chris, I felt worse about the gut shot on that buck than I did about putting down that sorry excuse for a human being today. That man, as you called him, was a child molester and a racist and was trying to kill my mentor and friend. And you'd rather French kiss a rattlesnake's asshole than shoot a shotgun at my friend Chris Caldwell."

"You'd rather what?" Chris asked while he was laughing

"French kiss a rattlesnake's asshole!"

"Man, now I have heard it all." Chris just chuckled.

"Seriously, though, Chris, I have no regrets and feel no remorse or pain from it. I will go to church this evening and pray to God for his forgiveness, but I will not apologize and I don't regret taking that shot. Really Chie—" Chris gave him a disapproving look. Trent smiled. "I mean, Chris, I am okay and won't lose a moment's sleep over it, but I thank you for your concern."

"Trent, I hear you and I would feel the same way. Still, I want you to see Dr. Coleman tomorrow and at least once a week for the next two months. If he tells me that you're okay after the two months, then I won't bring it up again. Call him, make an appointment, and you go on 'company time and the company's dime.' Understood?"

"It's a waste of both, Chris, but I'll go."

"Good, then. Thank you again, Trent, and tell Pastor King I said 'hello.'"

"Will do, Chie.... Chris... Will do, Chris."

Chief Caldwell gave an approving look.

With that, Trent Childress exited and Reggie entered.

"Is he okay?"

"He's good, Reg. Let's hear your theory."

"Okay, but don't call me crazy until you hear the whole thing."

"Gotcha. Knowing this case and what we have so far, I won't judge you until I hear you out."

"So, here it goes. I don't think it is one serial killer. As we both know, he would have to be nearly one hundred years old."

"Yeah, that's what you told me over the phone."

"At first, I thought it was a copycat or copycats. But I don't think that's the case. These cases weren't widely publicized and copycats need publicity. That's the only reason they exist. I think this is a family."

"I know I promised, but..."

"Please hear me out, Chief," Officer Hughes pleaded.

Chris nodded to his energetic young protege.

"I think someone, most likely a man, committed the original murder in 1937. Then, he taught his son to do the same. That is who carried out the 1947 murder and so on. So, our guy with these cases isn't nearly eighty or even ninety-five. He's great- or even great-great-grandson of the 1937 killer."

"That's your crazy idea?"

Reggie's mood changed from excited to unsure and he hung his head. "That's it, Chief."

"It's not crazy at all. Did you run this by the FBI?"

Reggie's confidence was quickly restored.

"No, I was waiting to see what you thought before I ran it through them. If this sounded too crazy to you, I didn't want to embarrass the Department."

"And you'd rather French kiss a rattlesnake's asshole than embarrass the Department."

"I'd rather do what?"

"It something Trent said. He said you'd rather French kiss a rattlesnake's asshole than shoot a shotgun at Chris Caldwell."

"I love that guy. That's hilarious and descriptive at the same time."

"Back to the subject at hand, Reggie, you have my blessing. Run it through them and see what they say. I'm calling it a day. Taking three sexual predators off the streets, albeit one dead, and nearly getting my head blown off with a shotgun is a full day, wouldn't you say?"

"I sure would, Chief. I'll see you tomorrow."

"See you tomorrow, Reg."

"French kiss a rattlesnake's asshole.... Now that is funny," Reggie commented as he walked out the door.

On the ride home, Reggie Hughes couldn't believe what was going through his head. Could there really be a family of men who seek and destroy families and kidnap their children? What do they do with the children they kidnap? Could they be stealing molested children and molesting them? Could they be part of other pods and stealing the merchandise of the pod? Could they be selling the children into sexual slavery? Why didn't they take more children? One every generation or so wouldn't generate enough money to make it worth the risk. If they were a member of the pod, they already had access to the kids. His theory was sound, but what was the reason for the kidnapping(s), the underlying motive?

Chapter 15
Why Not?

When he woke up the next morning, Brian couldn't get that question out of his head. Why did he only have to save one? He wondered, *Why just one?* "The Way" didn't dictate one. It just said they should pay it forward. This was a time to make a call that he both did and didn't want to make. He needed clarification on "The Way." His interpretation was that there was nothing to prevent saving more than one. If there was a rule in "The Way," he had already violated that rule by saving Rocky. But that was forgivable. To save the one, he had to save two. It was time to call Coach Horton.

Calling Coach wasn't a direct violation of "The Way." But it was something that was just not done. Once a child was rescued, raised, and reached the age of twenty-one, he was released into the public like a bird getting kicked out of its nest. The next generation didn't contact his rescuer with regularity unless there was an emergency or a special occasion. Also, the "grandson" of a rescuer could contact the "grandfather" if the father/son was no longer able to fulfill his duties (arrested, seriously injured, dead, etc.). To let the grandfather know who he was, the grandson would say "my chain is broken" and the father's name "said you can fix it." So, if Tyler, for instance, needed to contact Coach Horton because Brian was incapacitated, he would call Coach H and say the words Brian told him earlier: "My chain is broken, Brian said you could fix it."

As stated before, contact wasn't frequently made once the "baby bird" left the nest, so to speak. That was why Brian didn't want to make the call because his rescue and upbringing was more than he felt he deserved and he didn't want to add more to his plate, but Brian truly loved Coach H as a father and he looked forward to speaking with him.

Brian called Coach H. "Hey, Coach, it's Brian." Although their cover was father and son and Brian always referred to Coach Horton as his father, Brian never called Coach Horton anything other than "Coach."

"Young man, as soon as you said 'Hey, Coach,' I knew who you were. How are you doing, son? Long time no hear."

"Coach, I am doing great. I'd like to meet with you to do some catching up and talk to you about some family history. I have kind of a genetics question."

"You have a health issue that you're worried about?" Coach asked. He knew this wasn't the case. Brian was talking in code, which meant Brian thought someone might be listening in. Coach H was carrying on the fake conversation.

"No, I don't, but my nephew might have something going on that runs in the family."

So Brian has made his rescue, Coach Horton thought.

"Well, son, we can meet anytime. When and where?"

"How about tomorrow afternoon at our spot? Around 12:30?"

"Sounds good, son, I'll see you then."

Brian woke up the children and got them ready for their run. Today, they would step it up to one and a half miles. Time wasn't a concern, but he wanted to get their distance up a bit. His plan was to get them to be able to make one and a half miles without stopping, then work on speeding up the mile run. Once their time for that distance was under eight minutes, he'd increase their distance by another half a mile and continue this trend until they were able to run five and a half miles without stopping and, then, five miles in forty minutes or less.

After their run, he told them about the plan for the next two days. "I spoke to Coach H this morning." The kids looked puzzled. "Coach Horton, the man who saved me." The children gave a look of understanding. "Rocky, your question got me seriously thinking last night. I didn't get much sleep because of it, thank you very much."

"You're welcome." Rocky replied with a smile.

"Anyway, I don't know of a reason not to save more

than one. I need to talk to Coach H and I need to be sure I would not be violating a tradition that is over a century old. After you get a shower, we are off to the store to get clothes for Rocky. Then we are heading to Philadelphia. Have either of you ever seen the Liberty Bell?"

"Nope."

"Nope."

"Well, we'll be there tomorrow to check it out. Kids, when we get to the store, I need you to stay in the RV. People are looking for you and we can't afford to have you discovered. We need to change some hair color and length before you get to go out in public. Also, we need to let the heat die down a bit. A month from now, we should be able to move about fairly easily. Until then, we are playing a long game of hide-so-they-can't-seek."

Brian took the RV and the kids to the local department store. The kids stayed in the camper. He bought clothes to fit Rocky; nothing flashy, everything was nondescript. He bought a few pairs of jeans, some t-shirts, good running shoes, and some hiking boots. He also grabbed some blond hair dye and some scissors, a backpack, some food items, a metal match, and a CamelBak water container. Rocky's evacuation kit would be complete once he sewed some cash into the liner. Tyler's had been set weeks ago.

When they got back to the cabin, Brian exited the vehicle and started toward the cabin. Suddenly, he froze in place. His actions were so sudden that it scared the kids.

"What's up?" Tyler whispered.

"Do you hear that?" Brian replied.

"Hear what?"

"The absolute quiet. The only sound is the wind blowing through the trees. No birds. No cars. No dogs barking. Nothing. It's so peaceful."

Brian suffered from an overactive brain. Being able to concentrate and focus on one thing had always been difficult for him. He had never been diagnosed as being ADHD, but he imagined he was. His vast interests along with his abuse made his mind race from one subject to another. He didn't look at his racing mind as a hindrance. Instead, he focused on multi-tasking and used his racing mind to complete two or more tasks at a time. He could focus on homework while watching television or listening to the radio. In fact, he couldn't focus on homework unless there was noise in the background. He would write computer code while designing improvements to his electric motorcycle. But he always had to do this "multi-tasking." He had to play chess or something else on his cell phone while watching a television program to be able to "focus" on the show. But every once in a while, especially in the woods, his mind would go quiet and he could focus on the sounds around him. This was one of those times, but everything!! was quiet—his brain and his surroundings—and that was completely strange to Brian.

Then Rocky opened the car door and "to funky town, won't you take me to...FUNKY TOWN" emitted from the radio. As Rocky stepped out, she continued, "Won't you take me to Funky Town."

For some reason, this caused Brian and Tyler to burst into uncontrollable laughter.

Rocky paused. "Are you guys laughing at me?" she asked.

"No," Brian replied. "It was just the situation. Tyler and I were enjoying the absolute silence out here until you opened that door. Then... 'Funky Town.'"

Rocky got quiet. She stood still and listened. But it was too late. Birds started chirping and, off in the far off distance, they all heard a squirrel scampering through leaves.

With that, they all headed into the cabin. After three steps, Brian broke into, "Won't you take me to.."

The kids joined in. "...Funky Town." They sang all the way into the front door.

Once in the cabin, he helped both Rocky and Tyler dye their hair. Of course, Tyler was resistant, but he was pretty easily swayed with a quick "no questions" reminder. Once the kids were blonds, including their eyebrows (Brian was very detail-oriented) and Rocky was wearing a new set of clothes, he barely recognized them as their old selves and the kids barely recognized what they saw in the mirror.

The next morning, they woke up, completed their run, and grabbed some breakfast.

"Pancakes!!" celebrated Tyler.

"Yes!" exclaimed Rocky.

"There's turkey bacon in the microwave and I'm going to scramble up some eggs," Brian added.

"No eggs for me," said Rocky.

"Me neither."

"Okay, that's less work for me. Eat up; we're going to hit the road in thirty minutes."

Twenty-eight minutes later, they started their trip to Philly and Brian popped in a movie he had grabbed from the store the day before. This movie would be entertaining and educational.

"What movie is this?" Tyler asked.

"It's called *The Karate Kid*."

"I like that movie. Jaden Smith is awesome in it."

"Wrong movie, Tyler. This is the original version, which is better, in my opinion. I want you to pay attention to what 'Danielson' has to do for Mr. Miyagi and what he learns by doing it."

The drive to Philadelphia was uneventful. They had a brief stay at a rest stop along the way. There, they got out to stretch their legs. While walking around, the ugliest mutt dog approached Rocky. She looked down at it and said, "Aren't you the cutest thing." She leaned over and offered the back of her hand, the dog sniffed her and then licked it. When Rocky realized this pup was friendly, she began to pet it. The dog immediately rolled over on its back and Rocky rubbed her belly, which caused the dog's back leg to twitch continuously. Just then, the owner came up and asked, "Is she is bothering you?"

"No, ma'am. Is she always this friendly?"

"Yes, she is. I don't know what happened in her past. She was abused somehow, and when we first rescued her from the pound, she was a bit skittish. But after a few months of love and caring with us, she turned into this pile of ugly love."

"Ugly. She's cute," Rocky said with compassion in the tone of her voice.

"Sweetheart. I love this dog to death, but she is the ugliest dog I have ever seen."

"I find her cute." The next part, Rocky whispered. "Maybe she's so ugly that she's cute." Rocky smiled.

"Why are you whispering, sweetheart?"

"I don't want to hurt her feelings."

"Oh, sweetheart, she's deaf. That's why you didn't hear me call for her."

"She's a very sweet dog."

"Rocky, we have to hit the road," called Brian.

"Okay, I'm coming," Rocky called back. "Goodbye, ma'am. You have a good day. And what is your dog's name?"

"We just call her 'Dog.' She can't hear us, so it doesn't matter what we call her. So, we just refer to her as what she is. 'Dog'."

"Okay. Bye, ma'am and bye, Dog."

Just then, Dog let out a quick bark as if to say she understood the whole conversation and to say goodbye.

"Bye, Rocky," the lady replied.

Rocky hurried back to the RV and the crew drove off.

When they got to Philadelphia, Brian found a spot to park the behemoth vehicle. They caught a cab to Independence Hall. They had made it to Philadelphia a little earlier than Brian had planned, so there was time to do a little sightseeing. Brian wanted the kids to see where the Constitution was drafted. They were able to hang out there for an hour or so. Then they walked a block north and half a block east to Pat's King of Cheesesteaks to give the kids a genuine Philly cheesesteak experience. The kids loved them. Just before they got up to leave, a man who appeared to be in his mid to late fifties sat down at their table.

"I had a feeling you'd be here," Coach H said, surprising them. He looked at least ten years younger than his age of seventy.

"Coach, it's good to see you." Brian stood to give his rescuer, mentor, and FATHER a hug.

"Brian, who are your friends?"

"This is Tyler." Tyler shook Coach's hand. "And this

lovely young lady is Racquel."

"It's Rocky," she said in a correcting tone. "Pleased to meet you," she continued as she shook his hand.

"It looks like you guys were finishing up. Do you want to take a walk?" Coach asked.

They all stood up, cleaned off their table, and threw away their wrappers as they exited the restaurant.

Tyler grabbed his paper wrapper, balled it up, and shot it like a basketball with perfect follow-through and called out his fake NBA name, "Kobe." The paper bounced off of the edge and fell to the ground.

"More like No-be," quipped Rocky.

Brian and Coach couldn't help but chuckle.

The group walked out together, walked a few blocks, and passed Independence Hall and made their way to Washington Square Park. Once there, the two men sat on a bench and encouraged the children to "take a walk but stay in sight."

Naturally, Coach's first question was about two children and, in particular, Rocky. Brian explained the whole situation to him.

"...and I couldn't just leave her behind. I know it is against 'The Way,' but I just had to save her."

"Brian, son, I'm proud of you. I'm not sure I would have done anything differently. They already seem to be adjusting pretty well."

"Yeah, I'm waiting for the shoe to drop with one or both of them, but I think they support each other and I'm hoping that will make their transition easier."

"You may be right." Coach paused for a moment. "So, what's your concern about 'The Way'?"

"I'll get to that in a minute. Coach, I have a question about a different matter to ask you first."

"Shoot."

"Why did you wait so long to make your rescue? Were you uncertain as to whether you would do it or not? Was it raising the kids? What took you over thirty years to pay your debt?"

"What makes you think it took me that long?"

"Was there another?"

Coach went on to tell Brian about his failed attempt and how, in 1987, Coach H was a Lieutenant Commander in the Navy. He was stationed at Naval Air Station, Willow Grove in New Jersey. He lived in a town about thirty minutes away called Beattystown. In his neighborhood, there was a man, a little overweight and balding. Lieutenant Commander Horton always had a strange feeling when he saw the man. It had something to do with the look in his eyes. One day, Lieutenant Commander Horton was on his daily five-mile run, and as he passed by this man's house, he heard some screaming coming from inside the house. The screaming was obviously that of a child and the child kept yelling, "No, Daddy, I don't want to." He didn't know if the child was screaming because the father was making him or her wash dishes, pick up dog feces, or something far more nefarious.

Lieutenant Commander Horton stopped his run, slowly walked up to the house, and peeked into the house through a crack in the drawn curtains. What he saw made his skin crawl. The man had a child bent over a bed and the man was standing behind the child with his pants down. Lieutenant Commander Horton had a flashback to his abuse at the hands of his "father" and felt a sickness in his stomach that took him back some twenty years. He couldn't watch what was happening any more, nor could he hold down the English muffin he had for a pre-run snack. He turned to walk away from the window. His head was spinning between the rage inside and the desire to save this child immediately and flashbacks to his own days of torture. Before he could take his first step to take any action, his breakfast erupted from his stomach onto the rose bush below the window. The noise of his stomach vacating its contents caused a stir in the house just as a neighbor came out to pick up his morning paper. The neighbor yelled at the Lieutenant Commander Horton, "Hey, what are you doing there?" Lieutenant Commander Horton had no choice but to run away. A rescue would have to be made later.

When he got home, he couldn't get the vision of what he saw out of his head. He made plans to rescue the child that night. However, he was watching the news on the television that afternoon and he saw that man from the neighborhood addressing the press from a podium. The broadcast showed that the man was the New Jersey Commissioner of the Department of Banking and Insurance who had been convicted of taking a bribe but proclaimed his innocence. Lieutenant Commander Horton only caught the tail end of the press conference when the man made the statement, "Please make sure that this sacrifice is not in vain and tell my Drake that I am sorry." He stepped in front of the podium and pulled out an envelope to give to his assistants. Then he pulled from under his suit coat a .357 Magnum. Someone tried to move towards him and he said, "No, stop!! I don't want anyone besides me to get hurt." By this time, the man was standing just in front of the podium. He put the gun in his mouth and pulled the trigger.

In that instant, several things happened. First, his aide, who was standing behind him and just to the right of his right shoulder, was covered from her neck up in a fine pinkish-red mist of the man's blood as more blood and white brain matter were scattered all over the wall behind him. Also, the recoil from the gun that was no longer in the tight grasp of the man, since he was now dead, caused the gun to fly to the feet of the newsman sitting just in front of him in the front row. And, before that gun could hit the ground, the man's now lifeless body began to collapse almost like an accordion, straight down and slightly backward from where he was standing. Just after gun hit the floor, the man's body came to rest in the oddest position. He was sitting in front of the podium with his legs in a "crisscross applesauce" position with his upper body and what remained of his severely deformed and almost deflated head leaning against the podium. All of this occurred on live television.

The press assumed the last statement was because he was going to leave his children fatherless. Coach H knew otherwise. He saw in the paper the man had two children, one that was in college and one still lived at home, Drake.

"So you see, I found one by accident and, before I could save him, his father ended the misery. I followed up on the young man. He was around eight at the time I witnessed the abuse. Now he's thirty-three years old, married, and has two children. I check in on them from time to time to make sure the sins of the father aren't repeated by the son and, to date, they haven't... thankfully."

"Wow! Coach, I never knew."

"No one knew except me, the man, and, possibly, the neighbor. Missus Horton, I mean. Mom never knew, God rest her beautiful soul."

"That's incredible. I heard about that suicide at the FBI. I never knew the real back story. Okay, time for the reason I called you. Coach, Rocky asked a great question that we never addressed before and I don't know if our code, history, or tradition allows for it."

"Now I'm intrigued."

"Rocky asked why we only save one. In this case, I saved two, but I had to save two in order to save... my one... but why is it traditionally only one?"

"Brian, I'm not sure about this and I never really thought about it. My father, Chester, never talked about more than one. I don't think his father ever did. Hold on a minute."

Coach H took out his cell phone and dialed a number and put it on speaker. "Hey, old man, I have you on speakerphone. How are you doing?" He looked to Brian and mouthed the words, "My pops, Chester."

Brian heard his grandfather's voice for the first time in years. "I'm doing great, son. How are you?"

"Good. I'm going to have to get up to Boston and say 'hello' before you decide to make that one-way trip to visit your ancestors."

Brian could hear laughing and then coughing on the other end of the line.

"You mean, become one of your ancestors, but don't count on that happenin' anytime soon."

More laughing and coughing emitted from the phone, joined by Coach H's chuckles.

"Hey, I have a question for you... I'm sitting here with my son."

"How is Brian?" Chester interrupted. "Send him my regards."

"You're on speaker, you old coot, and he can hear you."

"Hey, Brian, how are things?"

"Pops, everything is great... better than great."

"So, you've fulfilled your obligation."

"Yes, sir."

It was Coach's turn to interrupt. "That's kind of what this call is about. Brian is wondering why it is always one and not more."

"It hasn't always been one. Adam saved many... rumor had it that he saved at least ten. To my knowledge, he only taught the 'The Way' to the first. Since then, we have only been obligated, so to speak, to save one. I didn't have the stomach for more and that may have been the case for my father and his before him."

"What you're saying is there is no violation in saving more?"

"No. But here is something to think about. According to my father's interpretation of Adam's teachings, if one of us saves a life, he is responsible for that life. So if you or your son saves someone, he is responsible for that person."

"What did Adam do with the other nine?"

"He took them to the Lakota, who raised them as members of the tribe. He checked in on them from time to time, but after ten or eleven years, each child was fully immersed in the tribe and it is believed that all of them stayed with the tribe."

"Thanks, old man. Give me a few weeks to get some things together here and I'll make that trip to Boston. Do you think you can hold on that long before visiting the ancestors?" Coach said jokingly.

"Son, like I said, I ain't going anywhere anytime soon. Hell, I'm going to outlive you. You'll be an ancestor before me, " Chester answered confidently and hung up.

"Well, son, you heard it. Adam saved nine after he trained the first in 'The Way.' So it has been done before. However, Yoda says you are responsible for any life or lives saved."

"Adam left the other nine with the Lakota?"

"Yeah, the Lakota raised them."

"Like foster parents?" he thought out loud.

"Kind of like foster parents," Coach replied. "What are you thinking?"

"I don't know. This is all fresh to me. But shooting from the hip, I'm thinking I'll train these two and move on to save others who are being molested. My only problem is what to do with the new kids."

"Are you thinking foster care?"

"I am, but I know how bad some of those situations can be."

"But are they worse than what we all have gone through?"

"You have a point, Coach. Are you saying I should do this?" Brian asked, seeking approval.

"I am saying you have fulfilled your obligation. We have all made modifications to 'The Way' from generation to generation. My grandfather introduced the trusty 1911. Before that, they used an old Colt .45 cap and ball six-shooter and Adam didn't use a gun at all. If you take on this new mission, you are modifying 'The Way.' That's all. And, you can do some good, but what will be the cost? And what will be the benefit?"

"I need to think this through. Let me ask you one thing?"

"Shoot."

"If I do this thing and get caught or killed, will you take up the mantle in raising these two?"

"Brian, that is our tradition. I have raised my two flesh and blood children and you. I think I can handle these two."

"I know that, but the risk will get higher than the norm if I take on this task. What I am asking is are you willing and able to raise these two if something happens to me while saving more?"

"Again, son, it is our tradition and it would be my honor to support you in that regard. You don't have to worry about anything happening to Tyler and Racquel should something happen to you."

"It's Rocky," Brian said in a girl's voice, to which they both laughed.

"When you've made your decision, give me a call and let me know what you decide. Either way, I'll support you, but if you choose to do this, I need to stop BASE jumping so I can be there if needed."

"BASE jumping? You're kidding!"

"Am I?"

Brian couldn't read him. Coach was always doing this to him. He had a poker face that couldn't be read. Sometimes, he would joke and Brian wouldn't have a clue; other times, he was telling the truth and Brian thought he was joking. This caused Brian to remember an event from when Brian was about seventeen years old. He walked into the house and Coach said, "What did you do?" Brian was puzzled. He had just come from hanging out with a few of his friends. "If you tell me what you did, I'll go easier on you, but if I have to tell you, there will be hell to pay." Brian stared at his adoptive father, trying to get a read. He couldn't think of anything wrong he had done... recently. Finally, after what seemed like an eternity but was actually ten seconds, Coach started laughing. The BASE jumping statement reminded him of that time. Was this old man really BASE jumping or was he "yanking his chain" again?

Brian and the kids bid him farewell and made their way to the Liberty Bell. After a look at the monument, they caught a cab back to the RV and started their journey home.

"Coach Horton seemed pretty cool," commented Rocky.

"He is very cool."

"What did you find out?" she asked.

"I found out that it's complicated. I need to think about this and formulate a plan if I am going to do this."

"You mean, if *we're* going to do this," Rocky corrected.

"So you're allowed to save more than one?" Tyler asked.

"I am, but it's more complicated than just saving more than one. Again, let me think this over and the three of us will discuss this later. Fair enough?"

"Fair enough."

Brian's mind was turning and turning. He tried to figure every avenue and result. He was leaning towards saving more but needed to come up with a plan. What would happen to those he rescued? He couldn't raise more than two or three kids on his own. He knew there were hundreds, if not thousands of kids out there that he could rescue. He couldn't save them all, and of those he could save, he couldn't train and raise them all.

How could he start to find the kids? The FBI was onto his remote internet hookup. He was going to have to quit his job in the very near future, so leads from his job would not be available. Should he even consider this? *I don't even have these two children settled in yet.* He tried to put the idea out of his head. He was trying to drive and think. This proved to be dangerous. He cut one unfortunate driver off and nearly ran another off of the road on a lane change. He couldn't devote himself fully to either task. *Damn you, Rocky,* he thought, amused. Finally, he was done. He was just overrun with exhaustion, distraction, worry, and confusion. He decided to call it a day. He pulled the RV off of the highway and into a rest stop. There wasn't much conversation between the three of them. The children could see that he was tired and preoccupied. Brian extended the slide outs to allow for the two forward sleeping sections to be used. He set the kids up for sleep and retired to the rear bedroom with his mind still racing.

Chapter 16
Finding a Phantom

Reggie contacted the FBI with his theory. When he spoke to the kidnapping specialists, they didn't find his theory crazy. They found it a bit unbelievable and forwarded him, oddly enough, to Agent Phil Hughes, the number two man in charge of investigating suspected serial killers.

"Deputy Hughes, may I call you Reggie? It's kind of odd calling you my last name."

"Not a problem, Agent Hughes. I understand."

"Please, call me Phil. I looked into your theory and each of the cases you found. Your theory is sound. It would be impossible for one man to commit these crimes. As for a copycat, none of the cases were widely reported, and copycats usually commit their crimes in a very short time following the original killings, not fifteen years or more later. A family training a son generation after generation is unheard of, but not impossible. Can I ask, how did you come up with this theory?"

"Well, my name is Reggie Hughes the Fifth. For five generations, the name Reggie Hughes with no middle name has been passed from father to son. Along with the name comes two things that each father gives to his eldest son on his eighteenth birthday. The first is the family's King James Version of the Holy Bible. The second is a Civil War era Spencer repeating rifle. Both are family traditions that take place every eighteen to twenty-five years or so, depending on when the next generation has a son. After looking at the cases, it occurred to me that this may be a similar tradition, no matter how sick it may be."

"First of all, if I am ever down your way, you have to let me shoot that gun. Second, putting two plus two together like that is pretty intuitive. All in all, this is some pretty good police work."

"Thank you. As for the gun, I shoot it every couple of months or so. If you're ever in town or nearby, look me up and you can put a couple of rounds through her. So where do we go from here?"

"That part is a little more difficult. If we had one of these killers from any generation, we could look up and down the line. So far, we don't have any of them. Our best bet is to find the latest one while the trail is still warm. The old cases are too cold. Given this new theory, I assigned some agents to look into the old cases to see if they are linked to this case in some way."

"Anything I can do to help?"

"Yeah, find the most recent killer. If you come up with something else, another theory, something to tie the cases together or anything, give me a call on my cell phone. If you ever get tired of small town police work, give me a shout. I'd love to have you on our team."

"You have the pull to do that?" questioned Reggie.

"Do what?"

"Hire someone for your team from off the street."

"Yes. I could hire you as a contractor, but even I can't make you an agent without the academy. However, I could cut through the red tape and get you in the academy in short order."

"Wow. Thanks for the invitation. But I like my small town."

"Again, if you ever tire of it, give me a call."

"Will do and thanks again."

"Talk to you later. Stay safe."

Reggie told Chief Caldwell about his conversation with the FBI. However, he left out the part about the job offer.

Chief Caldwell thought to himself, *I can't believe the FBI bought Reggie's reasoning. I thought they'd be more skeptical.* "That's great news, Reggie. What do they want us to do now?"

"Find the guy that killed the Creasys."

"Oh yeah, did I mention that I was walking my dog

last night and some guy just came up to me and said, 'I know you're having a hard time with this case and I just feel terrible about it. So you should just take me in because I am the one that killed those people,'" Chris said sarcastically. He was not trying to belittle his deputy; he was just frustrated with the Bureau, and Reggie was able to read that. He continued, "Seriously, the FBI wants us to find the guy. What in the hell do they think we're trying to do here? They're the world's finest law enforcement agency and we're a couple of "country bumpkins' and they want us to find him."

"Come on, Chief. We all want the same thing. What do you say we go back to the crime scene and take a fresh look?"

"Can't hurt. Let's go take a look."

Chief Caldwell and Deputy Hughes drove up to the property. Once there, they parked their vehicle at the entrance to the driveway and walked up to the house on foot. Chief Caldwell wanted to view the entire scene from the assailant's perspective. As he walked down the driveway, he noticed the tracks of a large vehicle, which appeared to have been parked near the entrance. "Did we note this before?" he asked his deputy.

"No, Chief, we concentrated on the inside of the house more than the outside. The FBI said something about the tracks belonging to a truck."

"Let's do our own investigation on these tracks. Grab the tape measure and camera from the car."

Reggie followed the chief's instructions. The two men measured the distance between both the tread marks from left to right and the deep tire impressions left in the wet ground from front wheels to the back ones. This would give them an idea of what type of vehicle it was, and just maybe, identify the exact kind of vehicle.

The two men were encouraged and walked more of the property to see if they could find any additional evidence on their assailant from the outside. After about thirty minutes of walking, Reggie discovered a spot where some tree limbs had been cut down and a blind created. The two men were avid hunters and had made similar blinds themselves when hunting deer. "Chief, call me crazy, but I think someone made a blind right here and it focuses on the house."

"Reggie, I believe you are right… on the blind part not the crazy part. Look here, you can see where a strap was used to tie something to this tree."

"A camera?"

"I'd be willing to bet your paycheck on it. This guy was stalking his prey, or scoping things out, before he acted."

Chief Caldwell walked directly from the blind towards the road. He tried to track the stalker's path to and from the blind. Just before he made it to the road, he found some motorcycle tracks in the soft ground. The tracks appeared to come from some knobby tires but not those of an off-road motorcycle. They were more like the tires used for an off-road/on-road motorcycle. He called Reggie over to the spot.

"Have Trent make a mold of these."

The two men walked up to and around the house. Reggie and Chris spotted it at nearly the same time. "Do you see…" they asked one another simultaneously. Reggie relented to his superior.

"Yes, Reggie, I do. There was something taped to this window."

Chief Caldwell took a few steps back and surveyed the rest of the windows on the house. He could see tape marks on two other windows on this side of the house as well.

"Reggie, look there and there," he said as he pointed at two other windows with tape marks. "You circle that way and I'll circle the other way. See how many more have the same kind of marks."

"Will do, boss."

"We'll meet at the front door."

Each man found another window, on either end of the basement, with the same marks.

"So this guy planned this thoroughly. He had a blind set up to watch the house and, apparently, had a camera pointed there. He taped something to five windows on the house. My guess is more cameras."

"Why so much surveillance? To plan the attack?"

"Probably so. My guess is this guy didn't want any

surprises. Let's take a look inside and see what else we can see."

Their investigation of the inside of the house didn't reveal anything new. They didn't find any new footprints or fingerprints. There was nothing out of the ordinary anywhere in the house except for the scorched bedroom.

"Reggie, I think we've had a productive day. I am going to compare the measurements of the vehicle we found to those in the database and see if we can find a match."

When he arrived back at the office, Chief Caldwell put the measurement of approximately 208 inches into the database. What came back started to make sense. The results showed a variety of recreational vehicles or box trucks. Chief Caldwell ignored the box truck results. This guy was sophisticated in his methods. A box truck was too crude for him. An RV made sense. It was a rolling hotel room, a mode of transportation, a kitchen, and a way to stay somewhere without much of a visual record. He needed to look at traffic camera footage for an RV with a motorcycle trailer or a motorcycle rack on the back.

He had Reggie contact Agent Hughes at the FBI to relay their findings. Hopefully, they could do a search of traffic cameras within twenty miles to see if any such vehicle existed. Agent Hughes agreed to take a look and get back to Reggie if they found anything.

The next day, Reggie received a call from Agent Hughes. "Reggie, how are you today?"

"Just fine, Phil. Better if you have something for us."

"Well, your day just got better. We found an RV with a motorcycle and rack on the back. It went through an intersection about fifteen miles away from the Creasy home at 3:12 a.m. the night the Creasys were killed."

"You're kidding me!"

"We couldn't make out the tag number on the RV, but we expanded our search and found the same RV on the security camera at a nearby LowMart. It arrived at, according to their timestamp, 11:06 p.m. and left at 12:03 a.m."

"Please tell me you got a tag number from their cameras," Reggie pleaded.

"Sorry, Reggie, we didn't. He seemed to have a coating over the plate that reflected camera flashes, but I have something almost as good."

"What's almost as good?"

"The guy got out of the RV and went into the store. We have footage of him walking into and throughout the store."

"Who is he?"

"We don't know. We never got a picture of his face. This guy knew what he was doing. He wore a baseball hat and never looked up. This is where you guys come in. Can you question the employees there, in particular the cashier, to see if you can get a picture of the guy? He went through checkout lane number 2 at 11:56 p.m. and paid with cash. We need you guys to find the teller and see if you can get a composite drawing of him, if she remembers him."

"Phil, we are on it. I am on my way into the chief's office now and we'll head directly to LowMart. I'll email you the composite as soon as I get it."

"Talk to you soon."

Reggie burst into Chief Caldwell's Office unceremoniously; so quickly and abruptly that he startled the chief, who nearly spilled his coffee.

"Chief..."

"Damn it, Reggie, you scared the crap out of me and I almost spilled my coffee."

"Sorry, boss, we have something."

Chief Caldwell looked puzzled.

"I just got off the phone with the FBI. Agent Hughes found an RV but couldn't get a tag number. However, they found the RV in LowMart down the street and the guy actually went in the store. They never got a picture of him, but they know he walked around the store for about forty-five minutes and checked out of lane number 2 at 11:56 p.m. They asked us to get a composite drawing if we can."

Chief Caldwell jumped up, grabbed his hat, and as he passed Reggie, he asked, "What are you waiting on, Deputy Hughes?"

On the way out, Chief Caldwell grabbed the department's tablet with the composite sketch app. A department this small couldn't employ a sketch artist full time; this was the closest they could come to having one. The app contained examples of each section of a face: the hair, the head, the ears, the eyes, nose, mouth, and chin. Using the app, one could get a fairly pretty good sketch of an individual and even add facial hair.

Once the tablet was in hand, the two men jumped into Chief Caldwell's SUV and headed to LowMart. With Deputy Hughes behind the wheel, Chief Caldwell was on the phone with "Nifty" Richie Gaines. Chief Caldwell and Richie Gaines played baseball and football and graduated high school together.

Richie Gaines garnered the nickname "Nifty" because of his moves on a football field. Richie could have been the cliché former football player. Until he blew his knee out in his senior year, he was on his way to the University of Memphis on a football scholarship. The knee injury derailed his plans to play football, but a year of rehab as a redshirt freshman allowed him to regain most of his form as a pitcher. He finished out his four years of scholarship baseball and acquired his Master's degree in Business Administration. He could have had any number of jobs out of town. He had offers from as far away as Seattle and a bunch throughout Florida. Instead, he elected to stay where his "Momma" and the rest of his family lived. It didn't hurt that the love of his life, Rebecca Smithers, lived there as well. In this small town, LowMart was the best option. He made good money there and had no regrets.

"Nifty, how are you, my friend?" Chief Caldwell asked.

"Just fine, Dumps. How are you?" Richie Gaines was the only person on the face of the planet that was still allowed to call Chris Caldwell "Dumps." Because of his size and bruising style of running, people called Chris "Dump Truck," which was later shortened to "Dumps."

"I'm good. How can I help you?"

"Friday night around 11:50, who was working Lane

2?"

"I'll have to look and see."

"If she's there, I need some time with her. We are looking for a suspect that came through her lane. If she isn't there, I'll need a name and address. I'll also need to talk to anyone there now that worked Friday night. Hey, Nifty... this is big. I know your people need to work, but this is a double homicide and a kidnapping. I really need your help here."

"You got it, Dumps. Anything you need."

"Thanks, man. I'll see you in a few minutes."

"See you soon."

The two law enforcement officers arrived at the LowMart department store. Nifty had already assembled those that worked Friday night in the lunchroom. Everyone who had worked that night was on shift except for two employees. Chief Caldwell thanked everyone for their cooperation in advance. He told them how important the investigation was. He showed them images of the man walking into the store, a few images of him throughout the store, one of him at the checkout, and one of him leaving the store.

"So please take a moment and try to think back to Friday night. If you came in contact with this man, any information you can provide would be greatly appreciated."

"Doris, that was your checkout lane that night. Chief Caldwell will want to talk to you first," Richie stated.

"Sure, Mr. Gaines. What can I help you with, Chief Caldwell?" replied Doris.

"Doris, I have this program here that helps me with drawing a person's face. I need you to tell me all that you remember so we can try to come up with a picture of the man," Chief explained.

"I'll do what I can, but there is one problem."

"What's that?" Chief asked.

"As I recall, he had a beard that covered most of his face and, if you ask me, it looked pretty fake because the beard was jet black and his eyebrows were brown. They didn't match... you know, the carpet didn't match the drapes."

"I don't think that is what that means," Chief

interrupted while trying not to laugh.

Reggie couldn't control himself. He chuckled.

"That's what my ex-husband used to say. Anyway, the beard looked kind of like that baseball player that had those commercials a few years ago, really dark and long."

"Like Brian Wilson?" interjected Reggie.

"Yes, I think that's his name. With that beard, I couldn't see much of his face. But those eyes. The eyes of that man are something I'll never forget."

"How's that, Doris?"

"They were gorgeous. He had the deepest blue eyes. They were hypnotic, and with his smile, even through the beard, and his politeness, I wanted to give him my phone number, even though he didn't ask for it and I am not that type of girl."

"I didn't think you were, Doris. Well, beard aside, you were able to see his smile. Could you make the outline of his lips?"

"Yes."

"Could you see the shape of his nose?"

"Why, certainly, Chief. Don't be silly."

"Well, you have those beautiful blue eyes, a nose, and a mouth shape. That will give us something to go by. It may not be precise, but it will give us a general idea."

"Like I said, Chief, I am willing to help in any way I can."

Doris and Chief Caldwell sat down with the tablet and went through eye shapes. Once those were settled, they went to the nose and on to the lips. Chief Caldwell inserted a beard like Brian Wilson's and, once done, Doris exclaimed, "That's him! There is one thing about his eyes, though, and I can't believe I didn't say this before."

"What's that, Doris?"

"On the bottom of his eyes, there were brown wedges."

"I don't understand."

"Okay, you know how the iris in our eyes is a circle, kind of like a pie?"

"Yes, Doris."

"Well, his blue pies had slices missing at the bottom

and the Good Lord replaced them with brown wedges."

"You mean sectoral heterochromia."

"Who's a... what's it?"

"Sectoral heterochromia. It's when one part of the iris, a sector, is a different color than the rest of the iris. Mrs. Caldwell has it. I think it's unique and beautiful."

"Me too. Especially in his dreamy blue eyes. Are you sure he's a killer and kidnapper?"

"No, Doris. I am not sure, but he's the only lead we have right now. Why do you ask?"

"There was something about him. Something in his eyes other than their color that showed kindness, not something evil. Still, those eyes were dreamy."

"Doris, I don't have a spot here for dreamy blue," Chief replied with a chuckle and a grin.

Doris blushed and smiled.

"Doris, you have been a tremendous help. Perhaps he isn't a killer, but we won't know until we find him. I thank you for your help. Unfortunately, I don't have Mr. Blue Eyes' phone number, but if you think of anything else, please let me know. My number is on this card."

"You're so silly, Chief. I'll call you if I think of anything. I hope you find him."

"I do too, Doris. I do too."

The two police officers took the rest of the staff that worked Friday night in groups of three to get their viewpoint on the suspect's appearance. Of the remaining staff, only two men could say they were able to get a good look at him. Their descriptions, however, were nowhere as detailed as Doris'. None of the employees actually spoke to the suspect and the men that saw him didn't see the beautiful eyes, nor were they taken in by his apparent good looks. They saw him as some "dirt bag" or "creepo" and didn't pay him much attention once he didn't appear to be a "lifter."

Deputy Hughes was on the phone with Agent Hughes as soon as they left LowMart.

"Phil, we are sending over a sketch of our guy now. The teller felt that he was wearing some sort of bearded disguise. She was taken in by his eyes, though. The program we have isn't in color, so I need to give you this detail. His eyes were, as Ms. Doris said, 'the most beautiful deep blue' and get this, he has that thing where the iris has a wedge of a different color."

"What thing?"

"What's it called again, Chief?"

"Sectoral heterochromia."

"Did you get that, Phil?"

"I did. I've heard of it before but never met anyone with it. Your email just came through. I'm going to put my sketch guys on this and get it in color. We'll run that through our database and see what we get."

Chapter 17
A Disturbing Call

When Brian woke up the morning, it was with a clear head and a plan. He had had a dream that night. In the dream, Brian was joined by a man dressed in traditional Native American garb that consisted of deerskin pants and shirt. This man was carrying a knife on a belt and a bow and a quiver of arrows. He had long hair down below his shoulders. In the dream, Brian referred to the man as Adam. The two men went on horseback from one house to another. In all, they "visited" four houses. At each house, they killed the parents in the tradition of "The Way" and they rescued the children.

The twist in this whole dream, the key that told him how and what to do, was something so simple, he was surprised he didn't see it before. The twist was the boy rescued from the first house went in the second house before the men. He went in to scout the situation and report back to the two men. After the boy reported back to the men what he saw, the two men went in to save the child. Then, the boys from the first two houses did the same at the third house and again at the fourth house. All of the children except for the first two were taken to the reservation to be raised as Lakota.

That was it; once the Tyler and Rocky were properly trained in "The Way," they could be his scouts. Children talk to children. Brian found Tyler by pretending to be another child. Secrets among children don't last long and any abused children would, hopefully, confide in either Tyler or Rocky or another child, and they'd hear it through the grapevine. Once the children had the information, Brian could run surveillance to verify the abuse and rescue the child, if needed. He would leave the child behind to be raised in either foster care or by an adoptive family.

His morning started as any other. He woke the children and had them get ready and they all went for their mile and a half run. When they returned, he sat them down and told them about his dream and how that indicated to him what was to be their plan.

"So you guys will be the intel and gather information."

"Spy kids, " replied Rocky.

"In a sense, yes."

"But we won't hurt anybody, right?" Tyler sounded unsure but relieved.

"No, Tyler, my hope is that you guys won't hurt anyone, unless you feel like you need to fulfill your obligation when you become adults. But if we do what we plan to do, I'd say your obligation has been met. It'd be your choice. You'll receive no judgment from me either way."

"Okay. So, if we do, that's cool, and if we don't, well, we've already done our part, right?" summarized Rocky.

"You got it! But none of this will happen until both of you have completed your training."

"How long will that take?" asked Tyler.

"That depends on you, but without going school and only home-schooling, it should take about nine months or so."

The children were excited to potentially play a part in saving other children but disappointed that it would take at least nine months before Brian would allow either of them to act on the plan. He used the Mr. Miyagi reference to quell their concerns.

Just before they got on the road, Brian received a call from his boss. "Hey, Brian, how's it going? It's Agent Ford." Brian could hear something odd in his voice.

"All is good, boss. What can I help you with?"

"Brian, we received a task from the homicide branch about a potential serial killer that includes that double homicide and kidnapping outside of Memphis. I know you are on vacation and I'm giving you another day on my dime for bugging you."

"Thanks, boss, but I spoke to Agent Martinez and I really didn't have too much to add."

"This is something different."

"What's up, boss?"

"We were able to get a sketch of the man from a teller at a LowMart nearby."

"How in the world did we track him there?" *What the hell did I do wrong?* Brian thought to himself.

"The local P.D. found tracks of a vehicle and a motorcycle on the property. They were able to match the length of the vehicle's wheelbase to that of an RV. Putting two and two together, they assumed the suspect would be driving an RV with a motorcycle on the back. Sure enough, we found one near the Creasy residence and leaving the area late that night and at a LowMart nearby about an hour before the killings."

"Wow, those guys are sharp down there." *I didn't count on anyone putting the two vehicles together.* "How can I help, boss?"

"We started to run the sketch through our databases, but it got hung up. We re-tried it five times and the same thing happens."

"Boss, what happens and when?"

"We put the sketch in, which is grayscale, and added the markers we know: brown hair color and blue eyes with brown sectoral heterochromia."

"Sector what?" *Damn, I forgot to wear my contacts.*

"Sectoral heterochromia. It's a condition or mutation where a sector or pie wedge of the iris is a different color. Anyway, we put that in the program and it spins through a number of contacts, but every time it gets to around record number 1873, the program crashes."

"That's odd, boss." *1873 and Sectoral Heterochromia—my trigger to stop looking because the search may result in the one result I can't afford: ME!* The crash was Brian's heads-up that he might be the suspect. A manual search could possibly lead to him, but he put a few precautions in place to, hopefully, avoid that.

"Did you try running it with just blue eyes?"

"No, we didn't."

"Try that first. I'll take a look at the program in the

meantime and see what I can find. Please have Agent Martinez allow all access from my cell phone's IP address and I'll hook up via secure access and see if I can find a fault in the program or database." *Good thing I changed my eye color to brown like my contacts in the database. Either way, I screwed up and they are close. Time to head for ground.*

"Will do, Agent Smart. I know you hate to answer these questions, but…"

"Give me about an hour. I should have something for you. This is a specific enough problem for me to track down."

Brian had the fix done inside of five minutes. *It's amazing how easy it is to fix a program when you knowingly put the mistake in it.* But he gave it forty-five minutes before he called back. He removed the sectoral heterochromia block. He added the option to put in the dominant eye color, the recessive eye color, and the clock position of the wedge for anyone with that mutation. With blue eye dominance and brown eye recessiveness, Brian would normally be discovered but not with his alteration of the database. He called Agent Ford.

"Boss, did you get a match yet?"

"No, we didn't."

"For this search, you won't have to start from scratch, but here's what I did for future searches. Continue with the blue-eyed sectoral heterochromia search as you have it. From now on, once sectoral heterochromia is selected, the tech will have the option to put in a dominant color and a recessive color and the clock position of the wedge. Since the database doesn't have this data in it for anyone entered before today, it will search for dominant color matches. They'll have to look at the picture manually to see if the sectoral heterochromia is present. All future inputs will have the sectoral heterochromia colors and the position of the sector available for both inputting a new subject and for searching. Searches for anyone in the database with that mutation will be easy."

"Damn, son, you are good."

"That's why you hired me, boss. Let me know if you need more."

"I think that'll do for now. Don't forget, you have an

extra day off. I'll see you Tuesday next week."

"See you then."

Brian knew he'd never be back to work. He'd have to resign fairly shortly. With the last access given to him by Agent Martinez, Brian was able to build a back door to the FBI's systems and, unless they were looking for his IP address to access it or someone stumbled on his back door, they would never know when he was in their systems. That was all he would need from the FBI in the future.

As for money, he saw a movie once, co-starring Jennifer Aniston, he thought. He couldn't remember the name of the movie, but the general premise of the movie was a group of bank employees come up with a program that would skim the round-downs from their bank. In other words, when a bank computes the interest on an account and it comes out to something like $50.644 cents, they round that number down to $50.64. The $0.004, or four tenths of a cent, is ignored. Brian tapped into three major banks. Those tenths of a cent were now deposited into various off-shore accounts to which Brian had access. These accounts had somewhere on the order of $10,000 deposited in them each month. He could turn on the program and turn it off as necessary to gain the funds he needed. That was how he paid for the RV, his electronic equipment, and what provided the "getaway" cash needed.

It was time to get off the grid. He explained to the children the happenings at the FBI and how they were uncomfortably close to him. The RV was compromised and they were going to have to switch vehicles. They were going to go to a truck he had stashed about fifty miles from them. Once there, they would need to gather as much as they could from the RV and transfer it to the truck. The windows of the truck were tinted and would hide them all for the last two hundred miles of their trip.

"When we get back, you guys are going to have to be restricted to the cabin and surrounding property for a month or so. I am going to have limited contact with the outside as well. Things are getting a little too close for comfort. Eventually, we're going to exercise our plan."

"OUR plan?" questioned Rocky with emphasis on the word "our."

"Yes, OUR plan. You're the one that asked the question that got the ball rolling. Tyler is the one that insisted I rescue you, and I am the one that formulated the plan. I'd say we all had a part in the plan and we are all going to have to play a part in its execution."

"No pun intended," sniped Tyler with a giggle.

"No pun intended," answered Brian. "We will find victims of abuse that the FBI isn't tracking and we will rescue them."

The new family of three made it back to their Virginia cabin without incident. Once back, they unpacked the truck and set up some of the equipment from the mobile command station in "Command Central." The next few days went according to plan and routine. Each morning started with a run of an ever increasing distance and a decreasing mile time. The children were getting faster more quickly than he had expected.

The Friday morning before Brian was supposed to return to work, he made a call that he dreaded making. He thoroughly enjoyed his job at the FBI and knew he was making a difference; however, the difference he was making was indirect. It was time he prepared for a more direct approach in making a difference. Of course, he couldn't let the Bureau know his true intentions. He would have to mask his need to resign in his recent need for a break, and he told Agent Ford, "I just can't take it anymore."

"Brian, please take a leave of absence of an unspecified length and return if and when you want."

"You'd let me do that, boss?"

"Brian, you are such a valuable part of this organization, we'd be stupid not to welcome you back at any point in the future, even if that is five years down the line."

"Boss, if you'd let me take such a leave of absence, I'm in, but I have one request."

"Name it."

"I can't be called for assistance anymore. Each time someone tells me about an incident, my skin crawls. I just can't take it anymore. It'll drive me farther and farther away."

"No problem, Brian. From the time I hang up this phone until you decide to come back to work, should you ever elect to do so, we will not call you, but I need one thing from you in return."

"What's that, boss?"

"Once a year on today's date, you need to call me and tell me you are alive. If you fail to make that call, I'll have to drop you from the books. Sound good?"

"Sounds good to me. Thanks for everything, boss. I'll talk to you in a year."

"Hopefully sooner. Take care, Brian, and be safe."

"Will do, boss. You do the same."

Brian hadn't counted on this response from the Bureau. He was out but could return if he ever desired to do so and, most importantly, they weren't hunting for him. This was the best of both worlds.

The first three weeks of training were going well. The children were running like white tailed deer for two and a half miles. They were getting to know their weapons with great precision. Tyler was able to make fire out of sticks, rocks, a bow, and some other "scavenger" methods. Rocky had become adept at starting fires as well, but she took to the magic of plants and how the oils of plants could be used to heal. She was able to use lavender to help with skin irritations and insect bites, the bark of a willow tree for pain and inflammation and things like peppermint and pine oil for muscle pain.

One day, the apparent happiness came crashing down. On one of their runs, Tyler stopped dead in his tracks and stood there looking off into the distance. When Brian realized what was happening, he turned back. This young man, Warrior-in-Training and abused boy, was nearly catatonic. He was staring off into the distance at what appeared to be nothing. Brian asked, "Tyler, what is it?"

"My parents abused me. They passed me around to kids, men, and women, and used me like I wasn't even a person. To them, I wasn't anything more than a toy. I loved them like a child is supposed to love his parents. I trusted them like a child is supposed to trust his parents and they treated me like I was nothing. I can't trust anyone. Not you, not Rocky. I can't even trust myself because my judgment and trusting led me to trust my parents and they did those things to me."

Brian had been waiting for this day. It was a day that all in the family line had to go through. Coach H had gone through it and Brian did as well. "Tyler, I understand. Don't trust me. Don't believe me. Look at me. Look in my eyes." Brian's eyes were starting to fill with tears. Rocky stood nearby but remained quiet. Brian could see the tears in her eyes as well. She was feeling the same pain. The same distrust. But Brian could see something else: the pain from Tyler's distrust of her and empathy. She felt for Tyler.

"Tyler, I have been abused by men, women, and my parents. I know how you feel. You don't have to believe me today or trust me. Hopefully, that will come with time. But look in my eyes and see that I know what you feel and I know what you have been through, not as an outsider looking in, but as someone who has been through it too. Know that there are two people here that know what you have gone through. One went through some of it with you and one has made it through to the other side. One day, you will trust again. You will trust me. You will trust Rocky. More importantly, you will trust yourself."

"They are dead."

"Who?"

"My parents."

"Yes, they are, and they won't hurt you or anyone else ever again."

"Why do I feel bad that they are dead and feel glad that they are dead at the same time?" Tyler said while sobbing.

"It's normal. You loved them and they are gone. So you feel bad. They hurt you and they are gone. So you feel glad. It is okay to feel both."

Tyler dropped to his knees and yelled out, "Why, God? Why? Why? Why did you let that happen to me?"

"Tyler, God didn't let this happen to you. Man did this to you. God sent me to free you."

"He did?"

"Yes, he did. There are two people you can't blame for these things. You and God. You did as you were supposed to do. You loved and trusted your parents. God sent me to rescue you from them when they didn't do what God had entrusted them to do."

Tyler got up and ran faster than Brian had ever seen him run. It was as if he was running away from his past or trying to run to his future. Either way, he was going to beat Brian to the house for the first time. Rocky followed behind.

When they arrived at the house, Tyler went straight to the bathroom to take a shower. Brian waited for Rocky. She made it to the house about thirty seconds after Brian, who was ten seconds behind Tyler. When she arrived, Brian asked her one question. "How are you doing?"

Racquel stood there for a moment and didn't say a word. Then, suddenly and without warning, Rocky started bawling like a baby. Brian walked up to her and hugged her. After a few minutes, Rocky's crying eased from a near hysterical out-of-breath cry to a good, normal cry. A few more minutes later, Rocky started talking. "Do you know how it started for me?"

"No."

"I had a bad dream one night. I guess I was nine or ten. Anyway, I climbed into my parents' bed like I normally did and cuddled next to my mother. Putting my head on her chest always made me feel safe. You know?"

"I do. My mother's bosom was once a place of comfort for me as well."

"That night as I drifted off, my father started touching me down there. I looked at my mother and she gave me this weird look. It was almost like a smile. That was all he did that night. The next day, he bought me an Xbox. I didn't know any better, but I thought the whole thing was very odd."

"Rocky," Brian started with a concerned tone, but he was interrupted.

"Well, the next night, he came into my bed and started touching me the same way. I didn't like it and it felt wrong, so

I jumped up out of bed and went to my mother's bed to hug my mom again. I lay there with my head on her chest, hoping she would comfort and protect me. My father came back in the bed and lay there. I could tell that he didn't feel right about it because he turned his back to us and I swore I could hear him crying. Then, it happened."

"What?"

"My mother…" Rocky was crying harder now. "My mother said to my father 'just do it, you little bitch' and he touched me down there and then he put his thing in me. The entire time, my mother was holding me. From that day on, I didn't know who to hate more, my mother or my father."

"Sweetheart, that's all over now. He is dead, and trust me, the police will have her within twenty-four hours. When she is in jail and the women of the prison find out why she is there, she will get what is coming to her tenfold. I am certain that God has a very special place in Hell for the both of them."

"I hope so."

"Use it," Brian told her.

"Use what?"

"Use the hurt, the anger, the sadness. Use it all to fuel you to be a better woman. Use it to become a weapon in body and mind. Use it to fuel your workouts. Use it to fuel your studies. Use it to make you love those that love you with that much more love." The first part of his speech was done. It was inevitably followed by a simple question. Brian waited for it, but it never came. *I guess part two will have to come later,* Brian thought to himself.

Chapter 18
The First Family Affair

After that one emotional outbreak by Tyler and the resulting conversation with Rocky, the children exhibited very little discomfort with their new situation. Tyler had one smaller outbreak and Brian grabbed him and gave him a hug. Then Brian reverted to a speech he once heard from Coach H. He later told him that the speech was part of "The Way," but it was as true for Adam as it was for Chester, Coach H, Brian, and the rest. It came in two parts. It was used only once in its entirety and later it was shortened to the first two words, if needed.

"Use it," Brian told him.

"Use what?"

"Use the hurt, the anger, the sadness. Use it all to fuel you to be a better man. Use it to become a weapon in body and mind. Use it to fuel your workouts. Use it to fuel your studies. Use it to make you love those that love you with that much more love." For Tyler, the first part of the speech was done. Just as he had with Rocky, he waited for the follow-up question.

"Is that what you did?" There it was. The question. Now it was time for part two.

"That's what I do every day. Tyler, I haven't forgotten what my parents did to me. I see it every night before I go to bed. I see it when I wake up. I see it when I see you. In an odd way, I miss my parents and grieve for them, but I hate them for what they did to me. I use the sorrow and hate to fuel all the good that I do and to make me a better man." The speech was done. All he had to do from that day forward was to say, "Use it."

Rocky was never given that part of the speech directly

because she never asked the "inevitable" question, but she was there when Brian made the speech to Tyler.

Racquel would sometimes cry herself to sleep at night, and every once in a while, she would just start to tear up. Either Brian or Tyler would notice and give her a hug. Those hugs along with the two simple words of "Use it" would cure what ailed her.

Nine months into their training, the children had exceeded Brian's goal of running five miles in under forty minutes. They were also skilled in hand-to-hand combat and were able to wield their weapons—a knife, a bow, and a hatchet—with great expertise. Tyler became efficient and deadly with the pistol. Rocky didn't like shooting a pistol as much. She could hit a man-sized target at twenty feet, but where she would hit on the man was a guess. Tyler, on the other hand, could call out "left eye" and hit him there or "nose" and place a bullet right where the nose would be.

They developed the plan for arriving in a new community and how they would start their time at a new school. First, they would look for a furnished apartment to rent. Once in town, they'd move into their new residence. Their cover story would be shared with the neighbors that asked. Brian was their uncle and the kids were siblings who were survivors of the car accident that killed their parents. Brian was named as their guardian and was the beneficiary of the life insurance policies. Because of the substantial amount of money in the policies and his job as a computer programming consultant, he didn't have to work to support the children. This freed up his time to care for the children, to make sure they were socially adjusted, and afforded him time to fulfill his dream of becoming an author.

Once they were established in their residence, they would report to school. Brian would bring transfer and medical records along with the children to register them for classes. After getting registered, tested, and placed in classes, the children would join clubs, find friends, and even try out for sports teams. The key was not to be too aggressive in making friends and to not do any investigating. They were to observe and take information volunteered to them by other students whether it be information about the student speaking directly to them or that student's friend.

After about a year of training and nearly three months of nagging from one child, then the next, Brian felt it was time to put their plan into effect. The three gathered up some clothes, equipment, and daily supplies from their hideaway in the Virginian Mountains and loaded them into the truck. They headed nine hundred miles west to a small town outside Tulsa, Oklahoma. Before leaving, Brian found a furnished three-bedroom apartment for rent and paid three months' rent in advance along with a security deposit. He hoped that would lead to a smooth transition once they arrived.

The trip took him less than the predicted fifteen hours, but they arrived in town far too late to move into their pre-arranged apartment. Brian took the children to a nearby motel. They registered and moved to their room. It was late in the evening, well past eleven. Brian and the children went to their room and readied themselves for bed. Brian took one bed and the children would sleep in the other.

Sleeping in less than three beds for three victims of child sexual abuse was almost humorously difficult. Brian had no temptation or desire to be with a child sexually, but he didn't want an accidental bump in his sleep to traumatize either of the children. The children had a history together and they didn't want to slip back into their past and Brian forbade it. Tyler and Rocky had devised a method to avoid slip-ups. They slept head-to-foot, with one child under the sheets and the other above them. This was a method that helped to prevent any urges they might have had from their previous experiences together.

They all went to bed and the children went fast to sleep, but Brian heard something that alerted him. Through the paper-thin walls, he heard sounds that made him very uncomfortable.

"No, Daddy, I don't want to," he thought he heard through the wall. He listened intently.

"No, not there, not again." The hair on the back of his neck was starting to stand up.

"Daddy, that hurts." Brian couldn't believe his ears. He quickly got out of bed, threw on his pants, and grabbed his knife. He could not let another child suffer at the hands of an adult with him right next door, regardless of the consequences. He slid out of the room quietly and peered through the neighboring room's window and peeked through a crack in the curtain. What he saw lowered his alerted stance. He saw a man and a woman, both of whom were, without a doubt, of adult age, being filmed by a man holding a cheap video camera standing at the foot of the bed. Oddly enough, he was wearing no clothes. Brian surmised that the trio was involved in some sort of amateur threesome video. There was no child abuse here. Although Brian assumed the female was probably a victim of sexual abuse at some point in her past, there was no need for anyone to die tonight. Instead, he returned to his room and turned the radio on just loud enough to drown out the noises coming from the room next door.

The next morning, Brian and the children started their day with a quick five-mile run. They cleaned themselves up. Brian asked a question to which he knew the answer. "Is anyone up for some pancakes?" He received a resounding "Yes!" from both children.

The trio went to a local diner for some breakfast. As they exited the vehicle, they noticed a man that looked disheveled. He approached Brian and asked, "Do you have a stick of gum, bro?" Brian was a bit shocked. He knew a question was coming but expected the man to ask for cash or food.

"I certainly do," Brian replied as he reached in his pocket and pulled out a stick of gum and handed it to the man.

"Thank you, bro. And since you were giving to me, let me be giving to you. Do you want to know how to live forever?"

"Huh?" This man's actions were so unpredictable that they really threw Brian off of his game.

"God gave me a message and said that I am King of the World and I can give the secret to eternal life to five people that I deem deserving of such a message. Your kindness and lack of judgment show me that you are deserving. There are two rules. First, If I tell you, you can only tell four people and the four you tell can only tell three and so on. Second, to receive the message, you must trust me and meet me at 231 Main Avenue at midnight tonight, no later and no more than three minutes early."

"Okaaaayyy."

With that, the man turned and walked away. Brian and the crew just stood there and said nothing. All three were stunned.

When he was out of earshot, Rocky said, "Something was different about that man."

Tyler replied, "Yeah, more than just homeless. That man seemed like he was possessed by the devil or something."

"Meth is the devil," Brian replied. With that, the trio entered the diner.

Once inside, they met a friendly waitress named "Kitty."

"Is that short for Katherine?" Brian asked.

"It is, but no one has called me Katherine—with a K— in over twenty years. Are y'all passing through?"

"No, ma'am, we are moving here. We arrived last night," Tyler replied.

"Well, then, welcome! I see you've met Charlie a.k.a. 'The King of the World.' He's a little different but harmless. I'm sure y'all will love this nice little town and the boys will love a pretty young lady like you coming to town. I'm guessing you two are in high school?"

"Thank you, ma'am, yes. I'm in the ninth grade and Tyler is a sophomore," replied Rocky.

"Tyler, it is nice to meet you. Pretty lady, what is your name?"

"Rocky... I mean Racquel, but no one has called me Racquel in years."

"I hear you, darlin'. Sometimes our nicknames stick better than our real ones. Frankly, I like Kitty far more than Katherine."

"And Rocky suits me better than Racquel."

"Rocky, what is this quiet and handsome man's

name?" asked Kitty.

"Ma'am, my name is Brian. It is a pleasure to meet you."

"It is nice to meet you as well. You have lovely children."

Brian could tell the woman was fishing a bit. "They are my niece and nephew and, yes, they are great kids."

"Look at you, taking your niece and nephew to breakfast. You must be their favorite uncle. Well, what can I get you to eat?"

"Pancakes," replied Rocky.

"Lots of pancakes," added Tyler.

"Let's start with three short stacks, a cup of coffee, and three OJs."

"Got it: three stacks, the oranges, and a java."

Kitty took their order to the cook.

"She seems nice," commented Tyler.

"And she really likes you," Rocky quipped.

"Uncle Brian and Kitty sitting in a tree," Tyler sang in a whisper.

Brian was a little upset at first, but he quickly realized that, no matter how much training they have gone through, Tyler and Rocky were still kids. All he could do was smile.

Ten minutes later, Kitty returned with the pancakes. There wasn't a word exchanged between this makeshift family. All they could do was enjoy the pancakes. When they were done, Brian thanked Kitty and gave her a seven-dollar tip on an eighteen-dollar tab. Either Kitty was impressed and appreciative of the tip or she really thought Brian was handsome because, before they left, she slipped him a piece of paper with her phone number on it.

The trio made their way to the apartment complex and Brian went into the manager's office to fill out the required paperwork. He was given three keys to the apartment and one key each to the amenities building and their mailbox.

They made their way up to the second floor apartment and went inside to check it out. Brian was impressed with the quality of furniture, appliances, and overall condition of the apartment. The kids were immediately impressed with the size of the sixty-inch flat screen television.

"That is awesome!" Tyler exclaimed.

The kids ran down the hall to look at the bedrooms. Tyler found the first room and called out "Dibbs."

Rocky made her way to the second room, which contained a canopy bed. "I found my room," she said happily.

They all continued down the hall to the master bedroom with a television mounted on the wall, a huge walk-in closet, a queen-size bed, and a separate bathroom. "Well, I guess this is my room," Brian said confidently. "Let's get our gear in here."

They moved all of their clothes and electronic equipment into the house. They used Brian's bedroom closet as command central. He would put his clothes in the dresser. Traveling light meant he wouldn't need the closet space for clothes.

Once they were settled, it was time to get to school. They jumped into the truck and headed to the high school. Brian took the fake transfer grades from a real school near Norfolk, Virginia and falsified medical records, which were fake records with their new names but their actual information. The dates of the shots were accurate to within a few days or weeks and any injuries they incurred were in the records as well, like Tyler's broken arm he had suffered at the age of two.

The children were given placement tests since they were coming from not only a different district, but from a different state. Both did exceptionally well on their tests and were placed in the appropriate grades; Tyler in tenth, where he'd be taking Geometry, U.S. History, English, and Biology along with his electives of P.E. and Spanish; and Rocky was placed in ninth grade, where she was taking Algebra, World History, English, and Physical Science along with her electives of P.E. and Spanish as well. In fact, they shared the same Spanish class. It was late in the day after their registration paperwork was done, testing was completed, and schedules were assigned. With only twenty minutes left in the school day, they were given a quick tour of the campus and shown where to report to homeroom the next day.

Not having an opportunity to go to the grocery store and having missed lunch with all the school paperwork, the trio headed back to their favorite place in town to eat, also known as the only place they had eaten in town, for lunch. Once at the diner, they were greeted by Kitty. "Y'all can't keep away from me, can you?" she said with a wink and a smile towards Brian.

That caused Tyler to hum ever so quietly the tune to Brian and Kitty sitting in a tree, to which Rocky giggled.

"Y'all take a seat anywhere you want and I'll be right with you."

They found a booth near the back of the restaurant and Brian took his customary seat where he faced the door. This was a habit he had formed by observing Coach H., passed down from generation to generation. The men in his "family tree" believed they needed to be able to see the door to be able to react to any ill-intentioned actions that might occur. This was a tradition that dated back to the death of Wild Bill Hickok, who was a gunfighter who believed in the same. Of course, there was always a possibility of someone who wanted to pay some ill will toward Wild Bill. One day, he joined a poker game and the only seat available was one that didn't face the door. He asked one of the players two times to trade seats and the player refused. Reluctantly, Wild Bill took the seat with the back to the door. Shortly thereafter, while holding a pair Aces and Eights, he was shot in the back of the head by Jack McCall. Because of this incident, the hand he was holding, "Aces and Eights," is now referred to as the 'Dead Man's Hand' and it was because of this incident, Brian always sat with his back to the wall or, more importantly, facing the door.

They all took their seats and grabbed menus from the menu holder. All three turned straight to the hamburger section, which was limited. The choices were either hamburger or cheeseburger and the cheeseburger had three choices of cheese: Swiss, American, and cheddar. Included with either was the choice of Freedom Fries (a post-9/11 holdout) or onion rings.

"So, newbies, what can I get y'all?"

Brian got his standard, a plain cheeseburger with Swiss cheese; Tyler ordered a hamburger with ketchup only; and, to the dismay of the males accompanying her, Rocky ordered a salad.

"A salad, that's not food. That's what food eats," Tyler said.

Kitty couldn't help but laugh. "I've never heard that before. Not food; it's what food eats. That's funny, y'all, but I guess it's because it's true. Two plain burgers, one with Swiss, one no cheese and a salad. The ketchup is right next to you, darlin'. What kind of dressing for your salad?"

"Italian, please."

"Okay, I'll have y'all's order up soon. Do you want those burgers rare, medium, or burnt?"

"Medium," Tyler and Brian answered in unison.

Kitty yelled to the cook, "Kill two medium cows. Make one of them swiss and fix a plate for an Italian rabbit."

The cook replied, "Two burgers, cooked medium, one with swiss cheese, and do what?"

"Give me a salad with Italian dressing."

"Oh, gotcha, a plate for an Italian rabbit. I like it."

They ate their meal. Brian tipped generously once again and received another piece of paper with Kitty's phone number on it.

She's persistent, if not desperate, Brian thought as he put the sliver of paper in his pocket with a grin on his face.

Just as soon as they exited the diner and were out of earshot, Tyler started whistling the same tune of "Kissing in a tree."

Rocky was more direct. "She likes you and she's cute. Why are you playing hard to get?"

Brian's head was racing. He hadn't been with or near a woman since he was rescued. Dedicating his life to "The Way" and staying busy at the FBI didn't allow for many relationships, either platonic or otherwise. In the back of his head, he didn't know if he could have a relationship, what that would look like, or how he would react to "normal" sex.

155

Would that activate something in his head and turn him into his parents?

"Honestly, Rocky, I don't know why."

On their way back to the apartment, they stopped by the local grocery store to stock up on food. Once they were settled in, the trio simply relaxed.

The next morning, the kids caught the bus to school. They made some quick acquaintances. Tyler found out that basketball tryouts were in two days and Rocky found that girls' softball tryouts were two days later than that.

In school the next day, Tyler was brought into the fold by some of the kids in his English class and Rocky made some friends from her Algebra class. They didn't meet anyone that demonstrated signs of abuse nor did they hear of any rumors of abuse, but it was early.

Weeks went by with no information or indication of any sick sexual behavior. Brian was starting to get discouraged in their plan. It was not that he wanted children to be abused, but he knew that there were abused children out there, and he wanted to find them.

It was time for some computer hacking. First, he looked back on their stay in the motel the first night. He found the name of the person registered next door. He did some tracing on him to see if any of his videos delved into child pornography and did a stakeout of his home to see if there were any children present. That proved to be a dead end. Next, he did what he was afraid or, rather, reluctant to do. He tapped into the FBI computer to see if there were any cases in the area the FBI was tracing. Again, a dead end. *Did I move us to the one town in America without any child sexual abuse?* he thought.

He was at his wits' end with this situation. He needed a moment to relax. A moment to clear his head. He needed to go out, but where? Who could guide him? *Kitty!* He looked through his wallet and found Kitty's number. He called.

"Hello?" an uncertain female's voice answered.

"Kitty, this is Brian. You know, with the niece and nephew from the diner?"

"Oh, Brian, how have y'all been? It's been a minute."

"We're good. We are finally settled in and have our routine down."

"What can I help you with?"

"I was hoping we could go out and get some coffee or a drink."

"Well, Brian, I don't drink. So a cup of coffee would be nice. When did you want to meet?"

"If you are available tonight, I'd like to see you. If not, whenever you are available."

"Brian, let me get something straight with you first. If you are looking for a—what do they call it?—'a booty call,' you are calling the wrong girl. I only gave you my number because I thought you were cute and I saw how much those kids adored you and figured you were a good man."

"Kitty, I am not looking for a booty call, and if you think that I am that easy, you are sorely mistaken," he answered with a chuckle.

Brian was not looking for a booty call. After all, he knew nothing about Kitty. He didn't know if she was the type of girl to move from "Mr. Right Now" to the next "Mr. Right Now" or if she was looking for "Mr. Right." He wasn't the man to fill either role. He was simply looking for female and, more importantly, adult companionship.

Laughing, Kitty replied, "How does Joe Schmoe's Coffee on Daisy Lane in forty-five minutes sound?"

"Sounds good. I'll see you then."

Before he could put his phone on the table, the children chimed in "Brian and Kitty sitting in a tree..."

"Okay, guys, I'll see you later tonight. Lock the door behind me and don't answer it for anyone."

"Gotcha, Lover Boy," Rocky replied.

"Seriously, you remember where the getaway kits are stashed, right?"

"Yes, Uncle Brian, we do," Tyler answered for the both of them.

* * *

Joe Schmoes was a coffee shop and diner combined.

Brian left and met Kitty. They grabbed a booth at the diner. Kitty liked to eat there when she was off. Her best friend, Tara, worked there. She knew the food was cleanly prepared, and she knew the menu and liked everything on it.

"Well, Mr. Brian, how do you like our fair town?"

"I like it. It's… quaint."

"That's one way to put it. Boring would be another." They both laughed.

"It's not a place to be if you are looking for some excitement, but the kids have had far too much excitement in their lives."

"What do you mean by that?"

"Their parents... the entire family was in a car accident. Their parents didn't make it. That's how I got them."

"Oh, that's so sad. But y'all look so happy together."

"Well, we are. We've been together for a little over seven years. So we have gotten pretty used to each other and have grown together as a family. At this point, they have been with me about as long as they were with their parents."

"The kids don't need any excitement. I understand that, but what kind of excitement do you like to get into?"

"Kitty, I am down for just about anything."

"Just about?"

"Kitty, I told you I'm not that easy," he said, laughing.

"Neither am I. Do you like go-karts?"

"I do."

"Well, let's go. You're riding with me."

"Okay. Let's go."

Kitty drove them to the local go-kart track and they had a good time racing. Brian even let Kitty win one of their races. Afterwards, Kitty drove Brian back to the coffee shop. When he opened the door to leave, she grabbed him and pulled him close and gave him a kiss on the cheek. "I had a great time tonight. Call me tomorrow and we'll find some more excitement."

"I will. I look forward to it."

Their nightly "dates" of excitement went on for about three weeks. They tried the go-kart spot a few times, saw a few movies together, and they even went to the local water park one weekend with the kids. While there, they all went down the water slides and rode the roller coasters.

While Brian was off on his three to four nights per week dates with Kitty, Tyler and Rocky were spending time with friends they had met at school. However, none of them found any evidence of molestation or abuse.

One night, Brian and Kitty met at their usual spot, Joe Schmoes' Coffee Shop, and Kitty asked him if he was ready for something different. "You bet."

Kitty took him to the local motel where she had rented a room. "I told you, I'm not that easy," Brian said.

"Well, I am," Kitty replied.

Brian and Kitty did something he hadn't done in quite some time and, for the first time, he did it without any guilt or regret or memories of his past.

After four or five similar meetings, they entered the room and the same man Brian saw through the curtain holding a camera that first night was there.

"What is this?" Brian asked. There was a look in the man's eye that just wasn't right. He had investigated the man that rented the room from their first night but didn't check the camera man out. This guy deserved a thorough investigation.

"I thought recording us would be exciting. We could watch it back. I think it would intensify our future experiences."

"Oookaaaaay," Brian was uncertain, "but does *he* have to record us?"

"HE is Hank West, and Hank records everyone in this town."

"What I am saying is can't we just mount a camera and use it to record us?"

"I guess we could. Are you uncomfortable with this?"

"I am. I'm uncomfortable with the whole video thing. Can we talk?"

"We sure can. Hank, I don't think we'll need you tonight, darlin'. I'll call you if we change our minds."

"I am just not into video recording of our... our

relations."

"That's okay. I was just trying to give you some excitement."

"What we have is exciting enough for me. Isn't it for you?" Brian asked.

"It is, darlin'."

"Well, let's not change anything."

"Okay. What about tonight?"

"I think it would be best if I just went home. I'll call you tomorrow, okay?"

"Okay, darlin'. Are we okay?"

"Yes, Kitty, we're okay. I am just a little freaked out about the video thing, but we're okay."

Brian left the room and got into his truck. He drove to the apartment and changed clothes into his all-black outfit. He barely said a word to the kids. Rocky was in her room and Tyler was watching television.

"Brian, is everything okay?" Tyler asked.

"I think I have a lead."

"Give me thirty seconds and I'll join you."

Brian thought for a moment. "Okay, son. Thirty seconds." Brian looked up Hank West's address.

He called me "son"! Son! Tyler thought.

In less than thirty seconds, Tyler emerged dressed head to toe in black, including his boots.

Brian thought to himself, *I have this kid trained well… he located his "ninja" suit and changed into that quickly. This kid is good.* The two "men" headed out to Hank's address while Rocky kept watch at Command Central. They sat at the end of his street and watched until the lights went out. When they did, they waited thirty more minutes. Then they made their move. Brian took the front of the house while Tyler took the back. As they had rehearsed several times, they planted cameras and bugs in each window of the ground floor and basement of the house. They left the second story of the house alone. As Tyler was moving through the backyard, he tripped over something odd. Away from the house, there was a manhole cover. It was in an odd location. It was away from the street where sewer drains were. He thought it might be a bomb shelter or storm cellar, but he couldn't find a way in, which seemed odd to him. Tyler gathered himself and, before he scampered to the front of the house to meet Brian, he planted a camera in a tree and trained it on the hole.

Tyler met Brian in the front of the house and, after they planted a GPS tracker on Hank's car, they moved stealthily to the truck. Tyler told Brian about the manhole cover and the camera he planted.

"Good job, Tyler. You did good, kid."

They headed back to the apartment and hooked up Command Central. Brian set the cameras to record. There was no activity. Since it didn't appear there would be anything important to see, Brian went to bed.

The next morning, he woke up and went straight to the video feeds. He saw that Hank was up and about. The basement feeds didn't show any activity and neither did the first-story house cameras. Where was he? The GPS tracking on the car showed his vehicle at home. Then he saw it out of the corner of his eye; the camera trained on the manhole showed movement. The manhole opened and Hank emerged carrying a bucket and two empty gallon water jugs. Something down there needed water. Hank walked over to a corner of his yard and opened another cover. This one was made of concrete and looked familiar. Once it was opened, Hank dumped the contents of the bucket in the hole. *He's dumping waste into the septic tank.*

Brian quickly rewound the video from that camera. There, he could see in reverse Hank emerge from the manhole again and enter the house. He stopped the rewinding and let it play forward. In normal speed, Brian could see that Hank was carrying a tray of food and a gallon of water. He knelt before the manhole cover and placed the contents of his hands on the ground. He moved a flower pot next to the manhole cover. There, he pulled a lever and the manhole opened; but just a crack. He lifted the manhole to its fully opened position and climbed in. Once he was in the hole a few steps, all that was above ground was his head and shoulders. He grabbed the food and water and went all the way into the hole. A few

Shane A. Ahalt Sr.

seconds later, the manhole closed. Brian fast forwarded the video and that took him to the point of Hank emerging with the bucket and empty water bottles. *There is someone in that hole.* He called the kids.

"Look at this." Brian rewound the video to the part where Hank entered and fast forwarded to him coming out and dumping the bucket. "There is someone in that hole!" Rocky exclaimed.

"I believe you are correct, young lady. I'm going to find out who or what is in there."

"How?" Tyler asked.

"It's going to happen like this. Rocky and I are going over to his neighborhood now. When he leaves his house, I'm going in that hole. Rocky, you are going to stay in the truck and listen for Tyler. Tyler, you will stay here and track his car. When he is heading home, you call me and let me know. Rocky, if I don't reply to Tyler's call because the cell signal doesn't reach or for some other reason, you are going to run to the hole and yell to tell me to get out. Whether I come out or not, you are going to run back to the street and walk quickly to the truck and wait for me. Got it?"

"Got it."

"What about school today?"

"You both are sick today."

Tyler coughed three times in a row. "Sick, got it."

Brian and Rocky left immediately. When they arrived in Hank's neighborhood, he was still at home. They sat in truck up the street and waited. Ten minutes went by with Brian sitting and watching and Rocky playing *Angry Birds* on her phone. They talked very little. Twenty minutes in, Brian, needed to speak. "What do you think is down there?"

"I hope it isn't kids or people. Can you imagine being stuck in a hole like that with a man bringing you your food and pooping and peeing in a bucket?"

"If there are people down there, the food and bucket thing is, in all likelihood, the least of their worries."

"Once again, you're right."

Hank's car left the driveway and headed down the street away from them. Brian called Tyler.

"Tyler, he's on the move. Are you tracking him?"

"I am. He's a quarter mile down the road and heading to the highway."

"Once he's on the highway, the next exit is ten miles down the road. That'll give us at least twenty minutes. Call me back when he's on the highway."

Three minutes later, Tyler called.

"He's on the highway."

"Got it. Thanks."

Brian made his way to the house. He strolled down the street as if he were on a daily walk. He observed all that was around him without looking suspicious. He walked right up to Hank's house like he was supposed to be there. Then he quickly moved to the backyard. Once there, he moved to the manhole. He moved the flower pot and pulled the handle. The manhole cover opened and he was immediately taken aback by the smell. It was worse than a football team's locker room. He looked down the hole for booby traps and cameras. Sure enough, where the third rung of the ladder should have been, there was tripwire in place. He could see that the wire was attached to a shotgun pointed directly at the ladder. Anyone stepping where that third rung should have been would have been shot in their side from their ribcage up to as high as their head, depending on their height. There were no cameras that Brian could see.

Brian made his way down the ladder and maneuvered his way around the tripwire. As soon as he got to the bottom, he made another scan. There were no other booby traps. He appeared to be in a buried sea train storage unit. He was at one end of a twenty-foot-long hallway. On his right was a wall. The left contained five cages. These cages appeared to be about four feet wide, eight feet tall and eight feet deep. Brian could see that each cage had a bucket and a cot and that was all it had for comfort items. Sadly, Brian could see the most important content of each cage was a person. There were three girls of twelve to fourteen years of age and two women that appeared to be eighteen or a little bit older. All of them were emaciated, dirty, and afraid. When the inhabitants of the cages saw Brian, they immediately turned their backs to him, grabbed the back wall of their respective cages, and removed their identical one-piece burlap sack dresses. Obviously, this was trained behavior and they were not unaccustomed to the presence of the other man or men in this hell hole.

Brian walked down the hallway to the far end of the bunker. At the other end, he could see a second sea train that was adjoined to the one in which he stood. They were joined in a "T" formation. Inside the second sea train, there was a film studio complete with a bed, cameras, lights, etc. It was obvious to Brian that these women and girls were the subject of videos made by Hank and, possibly, other men. What was also known to Brian was that this would not last another twelve hours. Brian moved to the ladder, and the girls put their dresses back on. He climbed up the ladder. Just as he reached the top, Rocky stuck her head in. "Tyler's been trying to call you. Hank's on his way back. We have about three minutes."

Brian climbed out and closed the manhole cover. Both he and Rocky quickly moved to the fence. Before they left the yard, Rocky stopped in her tracks. "The flower pot."

"Damn," Brian said as he ran to it and placed it back in place. They left the yard together and started towards the truck. Rocky held her phone up to her ear. "How long do we have?" she asked Tyler.

"About thirty seconds. A sprint to the truck will get you in the clear."

"We gotta run." They ran to the truck and climbed in. Once in, they ducked below the dashboard as Hank turned the corner. This time, he entered the street from the end where they were parked. He passed them and pulled into his driveway. "All clear," Tyler said.

They sat up, Brian started the truck, and they drove off. "Well?"

"It was worse than we thought."

"What could be WORSE than what we thought?"

"There are five girls down there. Three of them are in their early teens and two of them were about eighteen or nineteen. The two look like they've been there for a while."

"Have they been…?"

"Yes. There's even a studio to record it. I don't know how much of their original selves are left. Especially the two older ones. When they saw me, they didn't ask for help; they went to the back of their cage, grabbed the back bar, and removed their dresses. It's like different guys go there all the time and they are trained to serve them. They need to be rescued, but emotionally and psychologically, they are going to need more help than I can provide."

They returned to the apartment and filled Tyler in on what Brian had found and how Rocky saved his butt with the flower pot.

"This guy has to go. He has to go now. Tonight. Here's how we'll do this. Rocky, you are Command Central tonight. Tyler, you have the outside. You are going to get the cameras. Remember, there are six sets of them, two in the front, one on the west side, two in the back, and one trained on that manhole cover. Rocky, you will monitor the police scanner. If you hear anything that I need to know, you call me right away. Tyler, once you are done gathering the equipment, you go straight to the truck. You do not look in the house or enter it for any reason. Again, you don't enter the house for any reason at all!"

"Okay. Gather the equipment and get in the truck. Do not enter the house for any reason at all," Tyler repeated.

"We'll leave at midnight. We all need to get some rest. Go to bed. I'll wake you up at eight."

Everyone went to their respective rooms and took a nap. At eight, Brian's alarm went off, but he didn't need it. He was up, having never fallen asleep. His mind was racing about those girls. In particular, he couldn't get the older ones out of his mind. *Who were they? Where did they come from?* He jumped onto the internet, using his secure link for this one. He tapped into the FBI's missing persons database and looked for missing girls within a fifty-mile radius of their location going back eight years. What he found absolutely blew his mind. In the last eight years, fourteen girls from this very town had gone missing. *I have to be more thorough. I should have caught this before we even moved here,* he thought. He had focused on reports of abuse and failed to look at the big picture, a mistake he would not repeat. Three of those missing were runaways and were later found. Two went missing three years apart and were later found dead as a result of heroin overdoses, although their family and friends said the girls never used drugs. Of the remaining nine, six were assumed by the local authorities to be runaways because their home lives and relationships with their parents were tumultuous at best. Brian studied the photos of those six girls and he was fairly certain two of the girls were the older girls from the sea train. If he was correct, they had been in that hell hole for about five years.

The remaining three had gone missing over the last six months. They were all between the ages of eleven and fifteen. When Brian looked at their pictures, he immediately recognized them as the first three girls in the sea train.

This guy and whoever his accomplices were had been preying on the girls of this community for quite some time. By the looks of it, this had been going on for at least eight years. Also apparent to Brian was that once the girls were no longer of use, they were disposed of by overdosing them with heroin and dropping them off in an alley somewhere.

Brian woke the kids and they made preparations for this night. Brian double-checked his backpack, but all three of them knew it was already packed. Rocky checked the video feeds and saw that Hank was back in his house. He had made one trip to the dungeon, where he took food, which appeared to be peanut butter and jelly sandwiches, and water, and removed the empty water bottles and waste. Once he returned to the house at around 7:30 p.m., there was no further activity outside the house. Inside the house, Hank's activities were nothing exciting. He ate his dinner, took a shower, and sat in his recliner to watch television. He made no contact with the outside world and didn't show any indication that he knew someone else had been there.

By midnight, Rocky had been studying Hank's activities for four hours and reported "all is quiet on the Hank front." Brian and Tyler made their way to the truck and loaded their gear. The trip to Hank's neighborhood was uneventful. They parked the truck up the street and made their way to the house on foot. Brian went to the basement window and bypassed the lock on the window. In their research, the trio knew that Hank had no alarm system on the house. Brian surmised that was because Hank would rather lose items from inside than draw any undue attention to the manhole in his backyard. Once the window was opened and before he went inside, Brian whispered to Tyler, "Not for any reason. If I'm not out of here in thirty minutes, you drive the truck home, get Rocky, and make that phone call you have rehearsed over and over. Got it?"

"Got it."

"Six sets. Get all six sets."

"I'm on it."

Brian entered the house and closed the window behind him. He made his way upstairs to the first level of the house. He was careful in his steps. The booby trap in the dungeon had him on high alert. As he made his way to the steps that led to the second level of the house, he saw it. The same tripwire and the same shotgun setup. He stepped over it and continued up the stairs. Once at the entrance to the lone room on the second level, he made his way in, taser baton in hand. When he got to the bed, Hank opened his eyes. Before Hank could react to the threat he detected, Brian hit him with the taser. Hank went into convulsions and passed out.

Brian altered his methods a bit. There was no one for Hank to watch. No one else to torture. It would be all Hank and Hank alone. He zip-tied Hank's hands and feet to the bedposts. He stuffed a rag in Hank's mouth and duct-taped it in place. He took out his knife and looked at his watch. *Seven minutes in. I can't believe I'm on a clock.*

He used the skinning knife to skin the clothes off of Hank. Next, he pulled out his tomahawk and used it to crush Hank's left knee. Hank woke up, writhing in pain. "Hmmmm hmmm hmmmmm."

"I know. I know. You'll kill me. Yada, yada, yada. Look, Hank, I've been in your little dungeon. I've seen your work. I see how you prey on little girls. If I were to turn you loose, all that would happen would be a little more noise, as some furniture would be broken, but, in the end, we'd end up right here. Your actions have brought the wrath of God upon you." He used the tomahawk to flatten Hank's right knee. Hank flailed in the bed.

With that, he made a nick in Hank's chest with a knife and used the skinning blade to cut from his sternum to his navel. "Hmmmmmmm!" Hank screamed as the cut was made.

Brian did the same from each shoulder to each elbow. Both cuts received the same muffled scream reaction. Brian checked his watch. *Ten minutes in. Although I'd like this to last longer, it's time to finish up.* "Well, Hank, I'd love to stay and drag this out and, believe me, I could. You deserve my full time and attention and some very long suffering, but time is short. So we'll have to part ways like this."

With that, Brian skinned Hank from mid-thigh up and through his scrotum. "HMMMMM!!" Finally, he pulled out the gas, poured it all over Hank, and set him ablaze. After Hank had cooked for fifteen seconds or so, Brian extinguished the flame. Brian gathered his gear and exited the room, leaving Hank severely burned but clinging to life. On his way down the stairs, he stepped over the shotgun booby trap and took a moment to disarm it. He didn't want any first responders to suffer its effects. He took a quick look at his watch. *Fifteen minutes. Time to make an adjustment and call.* Brian quickly went out to the dungeon and opened the cover. He climbed down inside and changed the booby trap to the second rung. Any of Hank's associates would get an unexpected face full of shotgun blast. He exited the manhole and went to the truck. He didn't want the girls to suffer more than they already had, but he wanted to see if he could catch a rat in his trap. One more night in the dungeon where they were, while sleeping, would allow some space between him and his partner, Tyler, and the crime.

As they left the neighborhood and headed down the road, Brian asked Tyler, "Did you get all six sets?"

"Six? I thought it was five." Brian looked at Tyler in disbelief. Tyler saw his joke wasn't being well received. "Six sets. I got all six."

Brian cracked a little smile. "Don't play like that."

"I won't."

Thirty seconds later, Brian laughed. "Five! Dude, you're a trip."

They made it home and headed inside. Once inside, they listened to the police scanner. As the children sat around the scanner listening to it like a radio, Brian fell asleep.

In his sleep, he dreamt of Kitty. While deep in his sleep, he began to fall out of his chair. He was awakened by the falling feeling and caught himself with his hands as he hit the floor. The noise startled the children. When they realized what had happened, they laughed.

"What time is it?"

"Seven thirty?" Rocky answered.

"Did you hear anything on the scanner?"

"No, nothing about Hank. There were a couple of car accidents and a domestic violence incident at the motel we stayed at our first night here, but nothing on Hank."

"It's time for us to get those girls rescued. Where's the burner phone?"

"One step ahead of you," Tyler said as he handed Brian the phone.

Brian got in his truck and drove around the corner. He parked in a vacant lot with a "for sale" sign in it. He took out his voice-altering box, set it to make him speak in a deeper tone, and dialed 911. That call connected him to the nearest police station based upon the cell tower. He had to be quick. He didn't want a random police officer directed to his location.

"Listen closely," he said. "This call is concerning Hank West's house at 2131 East Rolling Stone Avenue. In the backyard, there is a manhole cover that leads to a hidden dungeon. Next to the cover, there is a flower pot. Move the flower pot and pull the handle. That will open the cover. Once inside, make sure your people watch the second from the bottom rung. It is a booby trap. Say that last part back."

"The second from the bottom rung is a booby trap," the operator responded.

Brian pushed in the truck's cigarette lighter.

"Good. Down in the manhole, five girls are being held captive. Hank is dead. Tell me about the trap again."

"The second from bottom rung."

"Good. Make sure the police know about the second from the bottom rung."

Brian pulled out the phone's sim card and the cigarette lighter. He used the lighter to burn up the sim card. On the way back to the apartment, he threw the charred remains of the sim card out the window. Once in the apartment complex, he took out the phone, wiped it down, and threw it in the complex's dumpster. He went to the apartment and straight to Command Central.

"They are already rolling to Hank's," Rocky replied.

"Did they say anything about the booby trap?"

"Not yet."

"If that dispatch officer gets someone killed…"

Brian was midway into his sentence when the broadcast came over the scanner, "All en route to 2131 East Rolling Stone, please be advised: The caller stated there may be a booby trap on the second rung of the ladder." Twelve minutes after Brian's call, reports started coming in from the scene.

"Dispatch, we are going to need an ambulance and as many emergency medical personnel as we can get on scene. We have one dead male inside the house, a severely injured female, and five additional malnourished females."

"One severely injured female?" Brian questioned out loud. "There were only five in the dungeon."

Brian and the gang listened to the scanner and heard the events of the day unfold.

"We're going to need the coroner over here and you better get Chief Halsey over here ASAP. He's going to want to be here for this. I have to believe the press is going to be here in short order."

"Will do, Vicki."

"Go turn on the local channel," Brian told Tyler.

About twenty minutes later, there was a breaking news alert.

"I'm Sue Carol, and I'm on the scene where the police

have made two gruesome discoveries. There is one deceased resident inside the house, an apparent victim of arson or an accident. Outside, another discovery has been made. At least five women and possibly one more were being held in an underground dungeon in the owner's backyard. The names of the victims are not being released at this time, but I am told two of the women have been identified and have been missing for at least four years. We, here at Channel Four News, will provide more information as soon as we have it. Sue Carol, WKEM, Channel Four News."

They all went back to the scanner.

"Ralph, did you find the chief?"

"Vicki, I haven't seen him. I tried his cell and it went straight to voicemail. Tried the radio, no answer. Any luck on your end?"

"I tried the same and couldn't get him."

"Vicki, try his vehicle tracker and let me know where it is. I'll head that way and inform him about the situation that is in progress."

"Give me a minute."

There was silence on the scanner.

"Ralph, give me a call on my cell."

"Will do, Vicki."

"There must be something seriously wrong with the chief," Brian said to the children.

The scanner went silent. There wasn't a word on it from the police, but the fire and rescue teams continued with their chatter. While en route to the hospital, they discussed the injuries to the woman. She had gunshot wounds to her left flank, shoulder, and left side of her head.

Thirty minutes later, there was another news break.

"I'm Sue Carol, and I'm on the scene where the police have made two gruesome discoveries. As stated before, one deceased resident has been found inside the residence here on East Rolling Stone Avenue. Apparently, he is a victim of arson or an accident. Police have also found six women in an underground dungeon in the owner's backyard. One of the victims, Katherine Meyers, suffered gunshot wounds and has been rushed to the hospital in critical condition. The names of the other victims are being held pending notification of their next kin. What we do know is that two of the women have been identified and have been missing for at least four years. The other three girls are minors and were reported missing up to six months ago. We are awaiting word from Chief Halsey. I am told a news conference is forthcoming. We'll break in with more information as we get it or when Chief Halsey comes to the podium. Sue Carol, WKEM, Channel Four News."

"What did she just say? Did she say Katherine Meyers?"

"Yes, Brian… wait, is that Kitty?"

"Yes, what was she doing there? I'm heading to the hospital to check on her."

Tyler asked, "Brian, is that smart? There will be police, cameras, news agencies, everything there."

"Tyler, you are right, son, you are right. Ahh, this sucks. Why was she there? This doesn't make sense. I know we weren't followed there."

"Brian, can I ask you something without you getting mad?" Rocky asked.

"What is it, sweetheart?"

"Could she be one of the 'rats' you were trying to catch?"

For a split second, Brian was livid, but then reason kicked in. She introduced them. She was the one that wanted the video. She was the one that initiated the relationship. Was she part of Hank's crew? Were they targeting Rocky? Was she going to recruit him?

"Rocky, sweetheart, you may be right."

There were no more news breaks all morning. Finally, there was one at two in the afternoon.

"I'm Sue Carol, and I'm on the scene where the police have made two gruesome discoveries. As stated earlier in the day, one deceased resident has been found inside the residence here on East Rolling Stone Avenue. The police are ruling it as arson at this time, pending further investigation. Police have also found six women in an underground dungeon in the owner's backyard. One of the victims, Katherine Meyers, suffered gunshot wounds and has been rushed to the hospital in critical condition and has been in surgery for the last several hours. The names of the other victims are being held pending notification of their next of kin. FBI Agent Willis is making his way to the podium to address the media."

"Good afternoon. I am Agent Willis of the Tulsa Regional Office. I can provide some information and clarification of the facts that we know at this time. The owner of the residence, a Mister Henry West, was found dead inside the residence. He was the victim of a homicide by a possible vigilante. Furthermore, police received an anonymous tip regarding a hidden shelter in Mister West's backyard. This shelter was used to hold five girls in captivity. Two of the women have allowed their names to be released. They are Miss Tiffany Randall, who was abducted four years ago, and Miss Sandra Canagra, who was abducted about six months later. Three more minor victims were found in the shelter. These girls have been missing for up to a year. The last person of interest is Miss Katherine Meyer. Although she is the victim of an accidental shooting, according the captive women, she was an accomplice of the homicide victim and was delivering food to the captive ladies in the shelter at the time she was shot by some sort of booby trap. I don't have any more information at this time but will take a few questions."

"Are the three girls Chelsea Ross, Rebecca Peters, and Brittany McDonald?" asked a reporter from a rival news channel.

"Ma'am, being that the girls are minors, I can't release that information right now," Agent Willis replied.

"Where is Chief Halsey and why hasn't he addressed the press?" asked Sue Carol.

"Chief Halsey's whereabouts are unknown at this time. Given the nature of the offenses here and the anonymous tip received, we are concerned for Chief Halsey and ask that should anyone see him or his vehicle, please contact the Tulsa Field Office."

"Are you saying Chief Halsey is a suspect in the homicide?" Sue Carol inquired.

"I am saying we are concerned that whoever committed the homicide here and called in the tip may have had some kind of grudge against Chief Halsey as well. We don't see it as a coincidence that he is missing at the same time this crime occurred. We are concerned for his safety, as he has been unreachable since this incident was reported. That is all for now."

"Well, there you have it. Five women have been found in Mister West's backyard dungeon. Two of them are long-time missing children, now adults, Tiffany Randall and Sandra Canagra. The three other captives are minor girls. Katherine Meyers, an alleged accomplice of Mister West, was also a victim of an accidental shooting and we have just been told she is out of surgery but still in critical condition. Finally, Chief Halsey is assumed missing and any information regarding his whereabouts is to be reported to the Tulsa Field Office. Sue Carol, WKEM, Channel Four News."

There it was; Kitty was part of Hank's crew or "pod" or whatever and Brian was sleeping with the enemy. Surely the authorities would be coming to question the man that had been spending several nights a week with her. The children's presence would raise questions he didn't want to answer. It was time.

"Kids, we need to break down Command Central. Grab as many clothes as possible and your 'disappear bags.' Fifteen minutes and we are out of here."

Tyler and Rocky didn't ask any questions; they followed Brian's orders and packed their bags. Brian went straight to Command Central and started to break down the equipment, but before he did, he noticed something odd... the GPS tracker attached to Hank's car was on the move. Twelve minutes later, they were on the road. They had no agenda for their next move, but the movement of Hank's car deserved some investigation, as far as Brian was concerned. So they followed it from about sixty miles behind. For the first few nights, they camped out amongst the stars as they traveled. Brian didn't want to have any sort of tracking on them. Four days later, they arrived in their new town, where the tracker had stopped.

Brian periodically checked in on the happenings surrounding Hank, the girls, and Kitty. Kitty survived the gunshot wounds, but her brain function was minimal and the prognosis wasn't good. The three girls were indeed Chelsea Ross, Rebecca Peters, and Brittany McDonald, all of whom were abducted within twenty-five miles of Hank's dungeon and all within the last twelve months. The investigation revealed videos of twelve to fifteen men and women involved in molesting the girls. One of those women was Kitty and one of the men was Chief Halsey.

The girls talked of a phantom man that came one day, walked to one end of the dungeon, turned on the lights in the studio, and then turned them off. He left, but later the same night or the next morning, they thought, he came back and moved the trip wire and left again. He never said a word, but a few hours after his last visit, Kitty came and got shot by the new wire and, shortly after, the police came to rescue them. The two adult women addressed the press on several occasions and, each time, they thanked their hero "Mister Phantom in Black." The parents of the three girls did the same.

Chapter 19
Time for a Vacation

The FBI's systems were hung up on the search for some time. Once their systems were in order, they came up with a few leads, but none of them really panned out. A local policeman on patrol in Pennsylvania found an abandoned RV. It appeared to have been gone through quickly. Much of the contents were gone. A bunch of electrical equipment was missing and wires were either pulled out or cut. The drawers were left open and the refrigerator was left open and empty. That was about all he could tell because the entire interior was scorched, or at least there was some sort of a flash fire inside. The FBI sent their fingerprint experts and they were able to come up with one single usable print. When they ran it through their database, it matched that of Racquel Williams, the kidnapped girl from the Tupelo, Mississippi case.

Otherwise, they left the RV without a trace and there were no other leads. Even the VIN showed the vehicle was registered to a shell corporation belonging to a Ukrainian business. The case was becoming a dead end. Chief Caldwell and Deputy Hughes were out of ideas. The Bureau monitored the "device" for nearly a year—to no avail. Apparently, someone had literally gotten away with murder, not to mention kidnapping.

***

"Reggie, I am beat," Chief Caldwell said.

"I hear you, Chief. It's time to call it a day."

"No, not today. This case has me beaten down. I always get my man and I haven't gotten this one. We even called in the world's greatest law enforcement agency, the FBI, and nothing." He said "the world's greatest" part sarcastically.

"I know, Chief, but something will give sooner or later."

"Son, we are almost a year past the 'First 48'," referring to the forty-eight-hour window that some believe makes the solution of murder or kidnapping cases exponentially more difficult to solve. "It has been over a year and we are nowhere on this case. And we don't have a clue as to who this Blue-Eyed Casanova is. This case has consumed me day-in and day-out and it has affected me doing my job. I have been thinking about taking some time off and Mrs. Caldwell is telling me that she needs me all to herself with no late night phone calls for at least two weeks. So I think I am going to take the next two weeks off."

"Chief, you have never in my three years on the force taken off for more than three days and that was only once."

"I know, Reggie. That's why it's time for me to take this well-deserved vacation. Do you think you can hold down the fort while I am gone?"

"Me? But Trenton has more time on the job." Reggie sounded unsure.

"Look, 'Mr. the FBI is recruiting me,' if you can't hold down our little town for three weeks, how can you make it in the FBI?"

"How did you know about...?"

"Agent Hughes called me soon after your first conversation to ask me about you. He told me he was impressed with you. I told him that you were still kind of green, but brilliant. I told him that you needed another two years on the job and then you'd be ready for the Bureau, and you will make a top-notch agent if that is what you want to do."

"Boss, I wasn't going to take the job. That's why I didn't tell you about it."

"Reggie, you'd be stupid not to. Look, there's still time to think this over. If the FBI wants you a year from now, you should take the job. You can always come back to this little town and be a deputy if you get tired of life in the big city, so to speak."

"Chief, let's cross that bridge when we get to it."

"Fair enough. So we are agreed. You're in charge while I'm gone."

"If that's what you want, boss. I'll take the reins while you are gone. But you said two weeks at first, then three weeks. Which is it and where are you heading, Chief?"

"Oddly enough, I think the Missus and I will rent an RV and drive across the country. Maybe go see the Grand Canyon and other sites along the way. Good catch on that switch-up. That's why I trust you to run the Department while I am gone. You don't miss a thing and nobody will be able to pull one over on you. It'll be at least two weeks but not more than three."

"Sounds like a pretty good trip. Are you taking your cell phone?"

"I am, but if you call me, the entire town better be on fire."

"Gotcha, Chief. Do not disturb the chief."

"That works for me. Look, I'll finish out today's shift and come in to clear up some things tomorrow morning. I'll also let everyone know that you are in charge."

The next morning, Chief Caldwell called the RV rental location nearby. He was given a "Chief's Special Rate" of fifty dollars per day with unlimited mileage. "Chief, you can't tell anyone about this deal. It's less than half price, but please tell all of your deputies about us. I'll give them a good deal—not as good as yours—but a good deal just the same."

"Sounds good. Can I pick it up this afternoon?"

"Sure can. How's four sound?"

"Four o'clock. I'll see you then."

Chief called a meeting of all his deputies, including those that were off for the day or not on shift.

"Ladies and gentlemen, I am taking the next two to three weeks off. I know none of you have seen me gone for more than a day or two or three, but I need to recharge my batteries. I have something like three months of vacation time due to me, so I am going to take a bit of it. This next part might rub some of you the wrong way, but I want your full cooperation in this. If I find that any of you cause Deputy Hughes any trouble, there will be hell to pay when I get back. Just in case you didn't catch that, Deputy Hughes will be in charge while I'm gone.

"Reggie, like I said before, don't you call me unless the town is on fire or Deputy Terry gives you any trouble." Deputy Terry, Reggie, and the chief all laughed at that one. Deputy Terry was Deputy Hughes' half-brother and best friend. There was no way he'd give Reggie any trouble.

Not twenty-four hours after he left, Chief Caldwell's phone rang.

"This better be important, Reggie."

"Chief, it is. Have you seen the news?"

"No, Reggie. Been kind of avoiding it."

"He struck again."

"Who?"

"Mr. Blue-Eyes."

"In our town?"

"No, just outside Tulsa. It's on every news channel out there. The FBI isn't letting this out, but he was dating a girl that was killed. When they went to interview him, he and his two kids were gone! One crazy detail… the Chief of Police in that town is apparently a suspect in the kidnappings. The shit has really hit the fan in that town…" Hearing Reggie use profanity was as rare as a woman not finding babies or puppies cute. He continued, "And I thought we had it bad here with the Creasy case."

"Did you say his two kids?"

"Yes, and a description of them sounds just like Tyler Creasy and Racquel Williams."

"Do they have any new leads on them?"

"Nope, they disappeared like phantoms again."

"Thanks for the news, Reggie. Is everything in town okay?"

"Yes, sir. Nothing to write home about or needing to call the chief about, but I thought you wanted to know about this."

"I did, Reggie. You stay safe and give me a call if the

FBI has any more information not reported on the news."

"I will, boss, but I'll leave you alone otherwise."

"Stay safe, Reg."

"You too, Chief. You too."

Chapter 20
Another Scouted Out

Once they arrived in their new town, Brian decided to keep things low profile. They checked into a small weekly rental motel under one of their cover identities. Once in the motel, they set up Command Central. The children were not enrolled in school and both were blond again. Brian now sported a beard, a real one this time. He had started it while dating Kitty because she liked "the scruffy look." Rocky's hair was shorter than it had ever been, but cute just the same, and Tyler just looked different with blond hair. Brian and Rocky couldn't get over how a simple change in hair color made him look so much different.

Brian did a preliminary scout of the address where Hank's car finally stopped via Google Earth. The property was very similar in layout to the Creasy residence. It was a secluded piece of rectangular property that sat far off of the road. The house was two stories and had a basement. The nearest neighbor was at least five hundred feet from the house. The distance would allow a shotgun to be fired inside the house without a neighbor hearing the blast.

The night after they arrived, Brian and Tyler went on a mission to install cameras at the property. They divided the tasks. Tyler would take the perimeter of the house where he was less likely to be spotted, and Brian, with his FBI credentials, would install cameras in the windows of the house. Brian installed a camera and microphone that would catch the activities in the living room and another set that peeked into the basement lounge area. The basement was like a scene straight out of the 1970s, including a few plush sectional couches, shag carpet, dark paneling with naked woman wallpaper above, and even a few bean bag chairs and lava lamps. Tyler installed cameras on trees at the corners of the residence to record those who came and went from the house.

Shortly after Brian installed the basement camera, a dog started barking inside the house. A few upstairs lights turned on and Brian had to make a hurried exit before he was spotted. Tyler joined him. From the sound of it, the dog wasn't really an issue. It sounded like a Chihuahua, Shih Tzu, or some other type of "rat dog," as Tyler referred to them.

On their way off the property, they cut through a wooded area and nearly ran into Hank's car. It was parked deep in some trees and covered with branches and leaves. Upon closer observation, Brian was able to see that the license plate was gone, the car was gutted, and even the vehicle identification number appeared to have been grinded out. Obviously, Chief Halsey or whoever was driving the car didn't want it found or identified.

While the men were out, Racquel was busy digging up information about the address on the internet the way she had been taught by Brian. She used the local tax information website to see that the property was owned by Patrick and Carla Loving. A basic search of Patrick Loving revealed that his wife Carla and their son Zachary also lived at that address. Zachary was thirteen years old. No other people were listed or associated with the address.

When Brian got back, he checked that the cameras and microphones were recording and he crashed for the night. The trip had been exhausting. That, along with the stress of wondering what Kitty was doing with Hank, how she was, and trailing a dead man's car and worrying about the safety of his two children (yes, they were his kids now) had taken a bigger toll on him than he imagined. Brian was beat and he collapsed on the bed and fell fast asleep.

When he awoke, the children had news for him. They observed Chief Halsey leaving and entering the house several times to smoke a cigarette. They also saw a teenaged boy leave the house to catch the bus for school and observed him return. From the outside looking in, everything seemed normal at the Loving residence aside from Chief Halsey's presence.

Inside the house, the conversations didn't appear to be abnormal. Zachary entered the house and went to his room and wasn't heard from most of the evening, which wasn't out of the ordinary in many homes with teens. There was discussion in the house of "tonight's party." For a Friday evening, that wasn't abnormal either. Around 6 p.m., a number of vehicles began to arrive. Some had couples, others had just men, and one vehicle, a Hummer H1, had a couple and another teenaged boy.

Here we go again, Brian thought. Unfortunately, his fears were confirmed. As he watched the video from the basement camera feed, he could see that the same activity that he saw over a year ago at Tyler's house was going on in this house. Zach was the "center of attention" and there were three other men present besides his father. There were also at least three women present, Zach's mother and another woman who was, apparently, the companion of one of the men, and another woman that was barely in camera view. He didn't need to see any more than what he had seen. Just as he was readying himself to get up and turn off the video, he saw the boy from the Hummer come out of a room escorted by the man and a woman from the vehicle. They seemed to be his parents, as all three appeared to be Hispanic. The three "new" attendees joined in the activities, although the boy was very reluctant, as was Zach. Once he had a clear view of the child, he captured a still photo of the trio. He hoped that it would help him identify the other boy or his parents.

Brian couldn't stand to watch anymore. He turned off the feeds from the inside of the house and kept the outside feeds on. He hoped to catch the license plate of the other boy's vehicle. About two hours or so later, he got lucky. The vehicle pulled away and gave one of the cameras set up by Tyler a perfect shot of the license plate. An inquiry with the DMV revealed the vehicle belonged to Mr. Paulo Alvarez. A check of his Social Security information showed that he had two dependents: his wife, Jezebel, and his son, Julian. It was time to double-up on the surveillance. There was only one problem. Brian didn't have enough equipment to watch two houses. He needed to find a way to watch a second house and buying a bunch of surveillance cameras might draw unwanted attention in this small town. Tyler came up with a brilliant idea. "Let's grab three or four cheap cell phones and use the Alvarez' own Wi-Fi to stream the feed to us."

Damn, that kid is a little FBI Cyber Crimes agent in the making.

"You know, son, that'll work."

Brian headed to the local mini-mart to buy a cheap GO phone with a camera. He bought a 200-minute card for the phone and paid for it all with a gift card he used like a credit card so as to not draw attention and to keep things untraceable. Rocky and Tyler each repeated the process over the next few days at different stores. Next, he drove by the Alvarez residence and checked for a Wi-Fi signal. Sure enough, they had a signal, but it was secure. Using a Wi-Fi hacking program he helped develop for the FBI, Brian quickly found the passcode to the family's Wi-Fi. A quick pause during a drive-by the house was all he would need to sync the phones to the Wi-Fi once he was ready to scout out the property. The drive-by gave Brian a quick lay of the land. Setting up surveillance at the Alvarez residence would be a little more difficult than the others because this house sat twenty-five feet from the street in a residential neighborhood with houses close on either side. What was easier for Brian was hacking the Alvarez' home computer and getting a live feed from the computer's microphone and camera that were always on. This hack gave Brian and the kids a little intel from inside the house.

While Brian was out, Rocky reviewed the audio from the surveillance at the Loving residence. When Brian got home, she filled them in on what she had seen and heard. The adults were already talking about having another "pod" party in two weeks.

"It looks like our time here is going to be very short."

"Are we going to save both of them?" Tyler asked Brian.

"We certainly are. We'll get Zach first. Then Julian."

Over the next few days, Brian obtained blueprints of

the Loving home in preparation for the rescue there. He would attack their home one night and, before word would be able to get out, he'd attack the Alvarez house the next night. But he needed to plan ahead, research each of the houses, and make sure that he planned for every contingency. Over the next two days, he would make the plans for the Loving and Alvarez houses while the kids bought their disposable phones to watch the Alvarez house.

While Rocky was out with Brian buying her disposable phone, Tyler was listening in on the Loving home microphones and the Alvarez computer and heard some disturbing news. Julian Alvarez and his family were moving in two days. He was not able to hear a reason behind the move, but there was no doubt there was going to be a move. A moving company had called to verify the move date. When Brian and Rocky made it back to the motel, Tyler filled Brian in on the move.

"Are we going to let him leave or are we going to save him?"

"Tyler, I haven't gotten the full plan together yet. I don't know how many people live there, what weapons they have, their routine, or any of that. A rescue at this point would be risky… Almost foolish."

"But we're going to do it, right?"

"We? If this is done, I will do it. You, Tyler! You will stay home and wait for me to make it back. You know the deal. You will be ready to get out of town if I don't return. Your 'disappear' kits will be at the ready and, if I am not back by 2 a.m. or you don't hear the code word from me by then or every hour I am gone, you disappear with Rocky."

"So you're going to do it?"

"I said 'IF'! and I mean IF. If I do this, Zach is going to have to be rescued quickly. Maybe even that night, but no later than the next night. That's going to draw a lot of attention to this area and, perhaps, us. New people that arrive in town check into a motel; they don't register for school; two families are killed shortly thereafter; two boys go missing and that newly arrived family leaves. Sounds kind of fishy, doesn't it?"

"It does. Maybe we can do it this way. Rescue Julian. Later that night, rescue Zach and disappear for months, only to re-emerge with new identities. You know, come and go like ghosts." Tyler replied.

"That'd be risky, but it might be our only option."

"So?"

"So, I'm going to think about this. Can I have ten minutes to think?"

"You can have five," Rocky interjected while giggling.

Brian weighed his options and there really wasn't a decision to be made. He had to save Julian and it had to be done tomorrow night. Immediately following Julian's rescue, he'd head to the Loving house to save Zach. He would leave the boys in a vehicle in front of Zach's house, drugged but safe, and ready to receive counseling and, hopefully, a proper home.

"Okay, get your stuff together. Load the truck with everything you want to take with us. Tomorrow night, I will save the two boys and we'll head on to our next location. How does Seattle sound to you guys?"

"I hear it's a wonderful city," replied Rocky.

"Home of Russell Wilson and the Seahawks," commented Tyler.

Always planning ahead, Brian started on their new identities. In their next city, they'd be Tyler and Racquel Adams, children of Brian Adams, although not the musician. Thanks to Brian's new backdoor access to the Social Security Administration, these were completely new identities created from scratch. Brian would have to fill in the school information from a Florida school system that he was able to hack, so no transfer grades from their last two locations would be required. Tyler and Racquel would be happy to know that they could return to their natural hair colors. No more blonde bleaching for any of them.

That day, Brian slept late in order to be well rested for the upcoming happenings planned for that night. That evening, he prepared his backpack with the usual tools: the baton, gasoline, chloroform-soaked rags, zip-ties, etc. He also took his trusty knife and the 1911 pistol passed down from generation to generation. He headed out in the truck a little after midnight and told the kids to stay awake, keep their phones charged, and be ready to go on a moment's notice.

Chapter 21
A Hurried Rescue

This rescue was going to have to be quick. He knew the family planned to move the next night and this child would be abused again somewhere down the line. Knowing that the abuse would continue for Julian over and over again, should he not be rescued, was too much to take. This boy had been through far too much, and knowing that he could prevent another night of abuse was enough for him to take the risk of a not fully scouted rescue. He would make a brief reconnaissance of the house. He waited until after midnight. Then, dressed in all black with backpack loaded and his knife and trusty pistol on either side of his belt, he made his way to the house. Once there, he scouted the house as a hunter stalks his prey.

No one was awake, and by peeking through the kitchen window, he could see the security system box and it was unarmed. That was one less step he would need to take. He made his way to the basement window, and with little effort, opened the window and stealthily made his way into the house.

The basement was a makeshift filming studio with a bed, overhead lights, a camera in front of it all, and even a sound boom. All of the equipment was top-notch. The floor was covered in shag carpet, but it didn't stop at the walls. That shag carpet covered the walls of the entire studio area.

He made his way to the stairwell, which also covered the same brown shag carpet.

This must be sound proofing, he thought.

He emerged from the basement in what appeared to be a "man cave" that was covered in Boston Red Sox and New England Patriots paraphernalia.

The rest of the upstairs was decorated with a more

modern flavor with none of that ugly green shag carpet. Oddly, there were very few family photos.

He made his way to his first destination, which was impossible to miss, Julian's room. The name "Julian" was mounted on the door in blue wooden letters. He pulled the chloroform-soaked rag from his pocket and placed it over Julian's mouth. The child fought for half a second, and then fell into a deep sleep.

"Step one complete," he whispered to himself

Then he moved to the parents' bedroom. His preparation and years of training had him ready for anything that could occur. Once in the room, he again used the chloroform rag; first on the father, Paulo. Although he was confident in his fighting abilities, the smart thing to do was disable the biggest threat. Next, he moved to the mother, Jezebel.

A fitting name for such an evil woman, he thought.

They were both in a deeper sleep and very unaware of the horror they were about to experience. He put hooks into the floor and tied Jezebel's hands and feet to them. Then he grabbed a chair that normally sat in the corner of the bedroom under Jezebel's vanity mirror and placed it next to Paulo's side of the bed. He then lifted Paulo's moderate-sized frame from the bed, placed him in the chair, and zip-tied his hands and feet to the chair.

He shoved another rag into Paulo's mouth and duct-taped it by wrapping duct tape over his mouth and around his head. Then he pulled out his tomahawk and used it to crush Paulo's left knee. Paulo was awakened by the pain but was still in a fog. He could tell that Paulo didn't realize his predicament just yet. To make sure Paulo was awake and aware, he brought the tomahawk down on his right knee. Paulo's agonized yet muffled scream let him know the fog had cleared.

He moved to Jezebel. He shoved a rag in her mouth and secured it with duct tape in the same manner and used the tomahawk to crush Jezebel's left knee. She was awakened from her sleep by the incredible pain. She screamed out, again muffled by the rag, in agony. He heard muted grunts, moans, and threats coming from Paulo. It was obvious that Paulo was now aware of the situation and was none too happy about it.

"You two call yourselves parents. A parent does not do the things that you do to your son. A parent doesn't allow others to commit the egregious and disgusting acts that you have allowed men and women to commit upon him. You are not fit to raise a child and you are no longer fit to live. You actions have brought the wrath of God upon you."

With this statement, he pulled out his knife and walked to Jezebel and, as he was readying to make a superficial yet painful cut, he heard a noise from what he thought was the basement.

No time to prolong their suffering. That's a shame, he thought.

He slit Jezebel's throat and moved, catlike, to Paulo. Jezebel was dead before he reached Paulo. He cut him from knee to groin, severing Paulo's femoral artery. This ensured his death would come within four or five minutes, but he would live through at least part of what was to come next. He then pulled the gasoline from his backpack and poured it over the two worthless members of society and, on his way out of the room, lit them with a match. The two bodies were immediately engulfed in flames. He went toward Julian's room, intending to take him out of the window. As he entered the room, he was welcomed with a blow to the head.

Stunned, he tried to figure out who or what hit him. He struggled to stay on his feet. He was losing that struggle. He fell to his knees and rolled to his back. Instinctively, he knew another blow was coming. To defend himself, he started to raise his arms across his face. As he raised his arms, he looked up between them and saw a familiar face. It was one he had never met in person, but one he had seen... in a sketch. The blue eyes with the brown wedges shone in the glow of the room, illuminated by the fire down the hall. "I'm a descendent of Adam too!" Chris Caldwell yelled out.

As Brian Smart was bringing the baton down for another blow towards the head of the man he thought was there to hurt Julian, he froze in place.